The Time of the Goats

The Time of the Goats

Luan Starova

Translated by

Christina E. Kramer

THE UNIVERSITY OF WISCONSIN PRESS

Publication of this English translation was made possible, in part,
with support from
the **Albanian Canadian Community Association of Toronto**
and **Canadian Macedonian Place Foundation, Toronto.**

The University of Wisconsin Press
1930 Monroe Street, 3rd Floor
Madison, Wisconsin 53711-2059

uwpress.wisc.edu
3 Henrietta Street
London WCE 8LU, England
eurospanbookstore.com

Originally published in Macedonia as *Vremeto na kozite* copyright © 1993

Published in France as *Le temps des chevres* copyright © 1997
English translation copyright © 2012
by the Board of Regents of the University of Wisconsin System

Printed in the United States of America

Library of Congress Cataloging-in-Publication Data
Starova, Luan.
[Vremeto na kozite. English]
The time of the goats / Luan Starova ; translated by Christina E. Kramer.
p.   cm.
ISBN 978-0-299-29094-8 (pbk.: alk. paper)
ISBN 978-0-299-29093-1 (e-book)
I. Kramer, Christina Elizabeth.   II. Title.
PG1196.29.T37V7413 2012
891.8′193—dc23
2012013019

Translator's Note

"Shared misfortune is less misfortune!" my mother said quietly . . .

Luan Starova (born in Pogradec, Albania, 1941), an Albanian who has lived most of his life in Macedonia, is a major Macedonian and Albanian literary figure. He was a professor of French and comparative literature, served as Macedonia's first ambassador to France, and is a member of the Macedonian Academy of Arts and Sciences. There is little contemporary Albanian and Macedonian literature available in English, and even less that treats Balkan history from Starova's multiethnic perspective. His multivolume Balkan saga provides a unique window into the Balkan twentieth century.

The Time of the Goats is the second novel in his Balkan saga. The first, *My Father's Books* (University of Wisconsin Press, 2012), introduces us to the narrator, who, following his parents' lives through the fifty-year period from 1926 to 1976, strives to untangle the family's complex religious, linguistic, national, ethnic, and cultural histories and to untangle the history of the Balkans, as new nations arose in the wake of the dissolution of the Ottoman Empire. The saga continues with *The Time of the Goats.* This novel-memoir opens in Skopje in the late 1940s just before the Tito–Stalin break and Yugoslavia's expulsion from the Cominform, the international Communist union. In the immediate aftermath of this political upheaval, local officials clumsily carry out absurd policies, dictated by the central Communist Party. In the ensuing political confusion, the residents of Skopje, the capital city of the Republic of Macedonia, face hardship and starvation as different levels of government enact laws that restrict the keeping of goats, leading eventually to the slaughter of thousands of goats. The father, an intellectual trying to make ends meet and keep his large family from starvation, befriends Changa, the leader of the goatherds. Together they try to help their impoverished neighborhood survive the years of postwar privation before the prohibition of the keeping of goats comes into effect, a policy sure to lead to more hunger, more deaths, and the loss of civic cohesion.

Tens of thousands of goats were, in fact, slaughtered in accordance with the law prohibiting the keeping of goats, promulgated in the *Sluzhben vesnik na Narodna Republika Makedonija* (see *Sluzhben Vesnik br. 88, god. IV*) on December 13, 1948. The reasons behind that slaughter are varied and multivalent: Were the goats slaughtered, as some claim, because of the depletion of forest lands? Were the goats slaughtered to strip wealth from wealthy landholders? Or was it, as others claimed, owing to Tito's plans for industrialization, collectivization, and the creation of an urban proletariat? These theories have been competing with one another for the past sixty years, and even today the controversy, and the line between fact and fiction concerning the impetus for this policy, continues, as the effects of that policy continue to reverberate.

In his novels, Starova draws on his knowledge of French literature. *My Father's Books* contains references to Balzac's *Eugène de Rastignac* and *Le Père Goriot*, the novels of Pierre Loti, and Camus's *Happy Sisyphus*.

In *The Time of the Goats* there is more extensive use of intertextual references, in particular to two quite different works: *Mr. Seguin's Goat* from *Letters from My Windmill* by Alphonse Daudet (1840–1897) and the *Book of Travels* by the Ottoman scholar Evliya Çelebi (1611–1684). Both works play a critical role in the plot.

Starova has won numerous literary awards, but *The Time of the Goats*, first published in 1993 and since translated into a dozen languages, has been the most enthusiastically received, winning, among other honors, best prose book of the year (Macedonia) and the Jean Monet award in the selection for the Best European Novel (France).

I am grateful to the following for their editorial assistance and advice: Ellen Elias-Bursac, Paul Franz, Victor Friedman, David Kramer, Madeline Levine, and Martin Sokoloski. For reference assistance I thank Christina Tooulias-Santolin at Robarts Library, University of Toronto.

In translating excerpts from *Mr. Seguin's Goat* I consulted the bilingual edition of *Letters from My Windmill*, translated by J. E. Mansion (London: George G. Harrap, 1900).

CHRISTINA E. KRAMER

Toronto, May 2012

The Time of the Goats

1

*A*s we put down roots beside the river, the fortress drew our gaze and took root deep in our souls. We often looked up from the stone quay toward the citadel, and our gaze would rest on the remains of the last war, the old cannons now fired to mark the important holidays of the victors: May Day, the Day of Victory, the Day of the Army, the Day of the Republic.

To us, new residents of the city, the fortress was like a balcony in the sky; it was the pride of the city. To reach the base of the hill with its towering citadel, one first had to cross the Wooden Bridge. Once across that wooden beauty, a veritable white palace came into view; its front facade jutted out, protected, it seemed, by a row of statues—caryatids— accompanied by a row of stone masks displaying every conceivable expression. This was the Theater, a grand old building constructed in neoclassical style that looked as if it had been pulled from Vienna, Rome, or even Paris, and transplanted here in the heart of the Balkans. With this new building and the nearby Army Club standing on the site formerly occupied by a mosque—known as the Burmali, or Spiral, Mosque—opposite the imposing bank building, with the main railroad station, which, in this minor Oriental outpost, was one of the most beautiful in the Balkans, the new state demonstrated its power. Indeed, now twenty years after the state's formation through the Treaty of Versailles at the end of the First World War, investments of foreign capital had established the symbols of power for this new era. These modern buildings, together with the old stone bridge and the large, towering fortress beyond them, famous since antiquity as a major stronghold of all the Balkan empires, gave the city its lasting appearance.

In the center of these buildings was a broad public square—probably the only one of such size in the Balkans—with one exit toward the stone bridge and another onto the main street that terminated in front of the railroad station. The most important train was the Orient Express, connecting the city with northern and western Europe as well as southern and eastern parts of the Balkan Peninsula.

The fortress—called the Kale, or "citadel," since the Ottoman era, when it had served as a large military barracks—was the sole symbol of those vanished empires. Each empire, doomed to inevitable collapse and oblivion, seemed to have its grave marker among the remains of the cyclopean stone blocks engraved with messages in different scripts, stone blocks constantly rearranged by new conquerors or tremors of the earth.

The inscriptions carved in the stones were worn away through time, releasing the history that had borne witness to the past. The time marked by those vanished civilizations rested on these massive walls. No force on earth could move them, except perhaps the catastrophic earthquakes that struck the city every five hundred years. Here, on this fortress, Balkan time had most clearly stopped. The inscriptions carved in stone by those former conquerors could, perhaps, be read as epitaphs of their former power.

After our great migration from our town on the western shore of the lake, we set down roots here by the banks of this rapid river, settling into an old, abandoned bey's house caressed by the shadows of four huge poplars towering high above the gap in which they grew, between the Wooden Bridge and the old Girls' High School, a school later given the name Josip Broz Tito; it suffered terrible damage in the last of those catastrophic earthquakes and was leveled, even though it could have been saved. In its place, a three-winged building—reminiscent of a pagoda—was built to house the Central Committee of the Communist Party until its collapse.

Only the Kale stood through time, though it too was shaken and damaged by earthquakes, and its yellow-brick barracks—which later became the Museum of the Revolution—lay in ruins.

After we had lived awhile in the city and the final vestiges of the war had been carted away, we children felt, after our defeats, an awakening desire or some vague instinct to conquer something. We would go past the theater and enter what was then the Jewish Quarter and would find ourselves at the base of the nearby hill, where, suddenly, there rose before us the cut and rippled clay belly of the hill. Its softer parts had been hollowed out over time—especially after drenching rains and river floods—creating deep, winding caverns, today's underground shelters for protection against bombardments and other attacks on the city.

Only atop the Kale could we view the entire city spreading from its center in all directions. Down below we saw the flowing of the shimmering dark-blue and golden-green waters of the river, and we felt as if we stood before the mast of a ship sailing through time.

We watched the people and old carriages go past, we gazed at the colors of the great bazaar and the eternal flow of the river. But no matter where we stood, it was the large square that drew our attention. Here was where history most frequently stopped off or passed by. Here in this square the first occupying forces halted, liberators announced their victory, mighty workers paraded, and important rallies were held.

One spring morning, when we had climbed onto the Kale, our eyes first turned, as usual, toward the square and caught sight of an unusual moving horde of whiteness completely filling the space. When we rubbed our eyes, we could clearly discern what was happening in the square below, and one of us called out, "There are goats, thousands of goats and people in the square!"

We looked in every direction, toward the far horizons of the city. Everywhere goats and people were flocking through the streets. A vast whiteness was assembling in the city square.

"It's a goat demonstration!" exclaimed another child, surely thinking of the frequent demonstrations in this square.

"It's not a demonstration but a goat parade!" chimed in a third child, recalling the frequent parades on the square.

Soon the square was jam-packed with goats and people. Renowned goatherds from mountain villages, who had led entire herds of nanny goats and vigorous billies, now made their way to the middle of the square and mounted the viewing platform, where, customarily, the highest leaders of the new Republic of Macedonia in the new Socialist Federated Yugoslavia stood during great parades, military processions, and demonstrations.

The goatherds waited onstage for their first meeting with the municipal rulers and the party.

What was going on in the square?

Above, on the Kale, we couldn't figure out what was happening, but it was clear that it was something big; the older children said it was something historic, something to be explained in the course of time.

The peasants who had not joined the "voluntary" labor collectives were heading to the city from the nearby mountain regions with their faithful goats; the authorities hoped that these goatherds would quickly form the working class required to fulfill the demands of the Socialist revolution. That is what was to become clear to us in the course of time. But how could we possibly make sense of all that?

The city was enlivened by the mountain air wafting in with its new inhabitants. It was with sorrow and regret that these people were leaving their native lands—lands that had brought them both good luck and bad. They had abandoned their native hearths, still hoping to return one day. Everyone took only the most essential possessions; they all took with them the keys to houses to which they likely would never return. It had been difficult to part with their chickens and especially their cattle, which were usually left with the collectives. In the end they had only their goats; no law or force of nature could separate them.

The goats remained, equal members of their large families. These goats had proved to be the saviors of many families during those long, hungry, and cursed years of war. Every family had several goat generations, with ancestors stretching back to other wars and other Balkan misfortunes. Without their goats, these people would surely not have survived to bring forth new generations.

Many of the goatherds' wives had, for the first time in their lives, dressed themselves in their wondrous folk costumes, dresses adorned with gilt threads and sparkling silver, woven in beautiful never-before-seen colors ranging from violet blue to yellow green, colors found only in the mountainous regions.

Their departure for the city marked a new, critical time for these families formerly scattered across the mountain slopes, down the mountain passes, and along the crests of the highest Balkan Mountains. Some traveled day and night to reach the capital city; others arrived within a day. Seemingly by mutual agreement, the goatherds had left their houses and mountain villages at the same time. It was clear that prior arrangements had been made. They traveled together, in columns. Larger families trailed larger herds of nannies, interspersed with a billy or two.

From time to time, the column would stop along the road when a child, or several children at the same time, could not stop crying. The goats stopped as well, prepared to nurse the crying children traveling alongside their starving mothers, who had not a drop of milk left to feed them.

The goats grazed on everything they found along the way: leaves, twigs, branches, grasses, anything remotely edible. They were moving reservoirs of liquid sustenance for those who, following the path of the victors of war, now descended on the main square of the Republic's capital. The goatherds and the does with their heavy udders marched on like the true victors in war. Along the way, they met soldiers, medals on their chests, exhausted from the long war, and young people volunteering on road crews. The goatherds stopped, exchanged greetings, and, with their natural mountain kindness, shared some of their last stores of goat milk and cheese. So it was on that spring morning that goats and goatherds arrived in the capital, welcomed by us children gazing down from our vantage point on the fortress.

Leading municipal representatives of the government and the party were well aware of the arrival of the city's new inhabitants, the yeast to give rise to a new working class, their class brothers.

They had expected that the newcomers would part from their native lands with difficulty and would arrive with a cat or dog, a chicken, a rooster, perhaps a sheep or two, maybe a goat, but never in their wildest dreams had anybody anticipated that the city would face a goat invasion. Nobody could believe—just days after the Day of Victory parade—that goats would be parading on the same square.

Representatives of the government and the party were thrilled with these new members of the working class who had bidden their final fare-well to their old life and mountain ways and would now surely strike the decisive blow to both domestic and foreign enemies of the working class. But now this "goat counterrevolution," this veritable white invasion, was blocking or, more aptly, destroying all the strategic planning of the party's main ideologues and thinkers.

The municipal leaders, accustomed to working according to the directives of their superiors—regardless of how much they might like to take the initiative—had no concrete instructions on how to deal with the goatherds and their goats.

Nor was there even time for quick consultations: the goats were here, and the goatherds, mothers, and children were all awaiting a swift decision. The city was confronted with—as it was later termed by several municipal party leadership cadres—"the occupation of the goats."

The municipal party secretary and the mayor climbed onto the reviewing stand to meet the goatherd leaders. The most prominent goatherd, obviously the leader, a man named Changa, wore a light goatskin cloak and a peaked goatskin cap shaped like Tito's partisan's cap. Changa was the first to greet the city leaders. He looked visibly puzzled by the party secretary's first words: "Welcome, brother villagers, builders of our happy future in a classless society. We have been waiting days for you, but for you alone, without your goats. Where did you think you were going with these goats, brothers? Do you think you will live and work in the city with them? Why, as the saying goes, one doesn't even go out to plough in the fields with goats—let alone in our classless society, in Communism . . ."

The leader of the goatherds, Changa, was a bit confused by these unexpected words of greeting. But when the secretary mentioned "Communism," he cleverly butted in: "Brothers, with our goats, we are coming from Communism, while you are just setting off toward it. Yes, we have been living naturally together with our goats in proto-Communist fashion. Together, we have shared our fates, we have been living with the goats in, as you would say, 'a classless society.' With our goats we came up against Fascism, and with them we survived. Yes, without our goats we never would have gotten here to join you, to become the working class together with you."

The nearby goatherds voiced their approval; the white mass shifted. The party secretary had not anticipated this reply. While he searched for an appropriate response, the whole crowd in the square shouted its approval, and nothing more could be heard.

News of the white goat invasion spread through the city. From the moment we first saw the goats gathered in the square, we children had run about the neighborhoods to spread the big news. At first, people did not believe us (it really was quite unbelievable); then they started pouring in from all sides, heading toward the great square.

Everyone had an interpretation.

For some, the goats announced the "white counterrevolution"; for others, the goats had come "because of the villagers' reactions to forced collectivization"; a third group figured, "Stalin was somehow mixed up in it."

By now, many people had joined the goatherds. When the goatherds quieted down, the mayor said to Changa calmly in carefully chosen words: "We expected you earlier. Trucks were arranged to bring you to the city. How did you get here?"

"Because of the goats we came on foot. There was no room for them in the trucks. And there was no way we would leave the goats behind," Changa quickly replied.

"I understand, I understand," continued the mayor with concern, "but what will you do now with these goats? Will you sell them, slaughter them, or . . . ?"

Changa bristled at these words. He wanted to grab the mayor by the throat, but he remained calm. His reaction was shared first by the goatherds, then spread to the whole crowd, to all the goatherds, children, mothers, old folk.

A ripple went through the white mass, signaling its disapproval, and seemed to send words directly to Changa's mouth. "The goats are a part of our families, our lives. Without the goats, we would be less, but with the goats, we are stronger. If it weren't for the goats . . ."

"I understand, I understand," the mayor interrupted in a soothing voice.

"You will never understand what the goats have meant to us . . . You will see their goodness here in the city!" Changa said, finishing his thought.

At Changa's words, the party secretary shook his head, signaling both skepticism and threat. He wanted to say something peremptory but restrained himself. Changa continued: "Respected citizens, look how sturdy our apple-cheeked children are next to your sickly, undernourished city children. Behind each of our children stands a goat: the rescued with the rescuer. These children of ours have mothers who gave them birth and goats that have kept them alive."

The party secretary and the mayor exchanged glances, not knowing what to do.

Changa did not mince his words.

The secretary thought that the goatherd's words were not in accordance with party norms. Had someone else uttered them, or had contradicted him in even gentler terms, he would certainly have been held responsible; he would have been shown his place, his place and those of the rest. It was unimaginable to hear such comments from the exhausted city residents, expressed in even softer terms—comments that publicly alluded to the regime, the party, the different classes, and Socialism.

The party secretary, seeking to regain the authority this goatherd was undermining in front of his subordinates, now turned and said to Changa in a calm and measured tone but loud enough so all the other lead goatherds could hear: "We are building Socialism on the path toward Communism, toward a classless society. This means that only united, combining the strengths of our peasants and workers, will we be able to build factories, roads, and bridges. We need heavy industry. We do not have dams, hydroelectric stations. Our cities are still not rebuilt; we do not have sufficient housing for our people. Furthermore, the houses we have are small, sufficient only for small families."

The secretary fell silent a moment to gauge the effect of his words; then, emboldened by the silence, he continued: "We found houses for all of you with great difficulty. We have erected prefabricated barracks. It will be a struggle, but we will be able to house all of you. But you have marched into the city with your goats . . . How can we proceed toward Socialism with them?"

No sooner had the goatherds heard these words than Changa categorically cut him off: "We are not taking a single step toward Socialism without our goats. We will go back with them from where we came. We are prepared to take them right back to our villages. As we told you, we survived there with our goats against Fascism, and with Socialism, as you say, it should be easier."

The party secretary first mumbled something under his breath and then fell silent. He did not want to get deeper into this conversation. He expected instructions. He did not want to risk too much, to lose any more of the authority that had been clearly undermined by these goatherds.

The mayor was a man along in years, careful, a man who knew the limits of his power, and when he was with the municipal party secretary face to face, he generally left matters to him. This time, however, it was immediately clear to him that he had to take the initiative himself. The orders from the central government, established by party directives, were absolutely clear: the goatherds were to be assimilated into the city, and under no circumstances should they be allowed to go back. On the contrary, that would mean accepting defeat.

This meant that he would have to house the goatherds with their families and—as events were unfolding—their goats. Such was the logic of the general directive.

The mayor made a swift assessment of what "his personal responsibility" would be if the goatherds left. He glanced over at the secretary. They understood one another.

The secretary was aware that the directive was confidential. He reflected once again on its content. He kept it in the large steel strongbox in his office, together with his revolver. The matter was clear. There was little maneuvering room. The mayor also grasped this at once, and he broke the silence: "Let us leave this discussion until later. We must understand one another! Let us return to practical issues. As we said, the houses designated for you are small. Each residence has several rooms. Each family has been assigned one room. Practically speaking, I do not see any space for the goats. We could lock them in several unfinished factory halls, or in the sheepfolds of the nearby cooperatives . . ."

The mayor racked his brain for several other locations where it might be possible to keep the goats, but Changa cut him off: "We are prepared

12

to sleep with the goats in whatever sort of rooms you've provided. Our children are accustomed to sleeping with them in the winter, to share their warmth; so are our wives and old folk . . ."

The mayor took the party secretary aside; they did not listen to the other arguments put forward by the goatherd. It was clear that the goatherds were not going to budge an inch.

The party secretary was furious, but he kept his temper under control. He was afraid of the directive's consequences for his career and possible retaliation by those whom he had criticized since taking power, with serious consequences for them. And there were many of them. Until now, he had never confronted such sharp resistance, not in the war, when he was a military commissar, nor after the liberation, when he was the leading figure in the city. He was losing control in these decisive moments, and he had to defer completely to the mayor. But Changa had him by the throat; he would pay for this one day. If only the damned directive had not been issued . . .

In a moment, it dawned on him that the directive applied solely to the goatherds, not to the goats as well. But he did not dare launch a new discussion with the goatherds, because he would find himself once again in a hopeless position. Yes, the instructions related to the goatherds, not to those damned white devils who could easily jeopardize his career.

He tried not to say anything to endanger his authority further. He briefly considered convening the elite municipal party leadership in order to spread the responsibility around, but there was no time, nor was he certain it would be effective. There were additional military and police forces, but in order to call them in, it would be necessary to have urgent consultation with all levels of party structures in the republic. He was afraid of doing that. The task, therefore, would be delegated to the mayor and his executive committee.

Nightfall slowly descended on the city. In the distance, lights were being lit on the fortress. The goatherds and their goats did not leave the square. Their children gave the goats the last of the dried leaves they had gathered along the way.

The party secretary and the mayor called together the authorities in the municipal government and members of the party's central committee. A temporary measure was introduced to house the goatherds with their goats in the requisitioned houses and apartments; the problem with the goats would be resolved in accordance with the instructions they anticipated would come down from the higher party executive. However, all those present were firmly convinced—and voiced this opinion more than once—that the goatherds, once they saw what awaited them, would quickly decide to relinquish the goats.

Much later that night, the party secretary and the mayor returned to the square with their trusted assistants to inform Changa and the other goatherds of their decision to allow them to reside temporarily with their goats in the housing the city had requisitioned for them.

The younger children had already fallen asleep curled among the goats, warmed by their bodies. The mothers, happy that their children were sleeping, were preparing food from the last crumbs remaining in their sacks.

Suddenly, a noisy commotion erupted in the square.

The goatherds began to celebrate their first victory in the city. A revolutionary song, with goats now inserted into the lyrics, burst forth. The children awoke in tears, frightened. The happy shouts, the children's crying, and the bleating of the goats jumbled together.

The white column made its way through the city and disappeared into the many empty houses.

2

*I*n the city, the time of the goats set in.

When the villagers arrived with their goats, the city natives viewed them with fear, suspicious that they would divide the cake of hunger into ever smaller pieces until they all starved.

But that is not what happened!

The goatherds soon found their way in the city. They organized the space in the abandoned, half-empty houses. They constructed sheds next to the houses for their goats and for the storage of leaves and hay.

In the course of time, the older city residents, especially those who bore the brunt of the "class struggle" and those from whom nearly everything had been taken by the new government, started to befriend the goatherds. There were, as well, some prominent officials in the new government who were understanding of the goatherds and their goats. They had many children but little pay and found it difficult to make ends meet in those days of poverty; they bought inexpensive milk from the goatherds, even though the government and the party followed their every move.

There could be no doubt. The goats had taken over the city. Soon the children's liveliness returned; they walked with a firmer step, kept longer at their games, and made greater progress in school. But to everyone's dismay, except some of the hard-core party ideologues, the time allotted by the party and the government for the goats to remain in the city was quickly passing. The central committee outlined an agreement, which was, eventually, discreetly passed on to Changa: the goats had to be either returned to the villages, where they would be slaughtered, or handed over to be served up here in workers' cafeterias. With the exception of a small number of zealous party cadres, everybody—including junior and senior officials—procured goat milk and other dairy products on the sly, so others would not see them. Some of the junior cadres were punished, but a blind eye was turned to the actions of senior officials. For the holidays, Changa sent a barrel of high-quality goat cheese to the party secretary and the mayor. Everybody in the capital city of this southern republic kept quiet, caught in the spider's web spun by the "goat mafia," as the true-believing ideologues called it—mainly among themselves.

The country had been beset by years of poverty and hunger. The Cold War had begun a few years after the war against Fascism, which had affected many countries. The events of history took their toll. The farming and livestock collectives did not meet their quotas. Little food was produced in the cities. The peasants were resisting transformation into a working class. The reparations after the war; the forced collective labor; shock-worker badges, medals, and slogans had produced few results. The planned factories, schools, roads, and bridges could not be built. Hunger rapped on the doors of nearly every family. But the party's directives for the future were categorical: once the class enemy was completely crushed, the working class must be created.

All the party leaders in the city—who had received the secret directive for the transformation of the goatherds (countless numbers across the country) into the "working class"—felt the hunger, but they also felt the good fortune flowing from the goatherds' clever moves and were in constant fear that another executive directive would arrive seeking the final liquidation of every goat in the country.

Everyone feared that fateful directive, one of a long line of them, which would mean the end not only to the goats but also to the vitality returning to the people's faces for the first time since the war, in freedom.

Along with international food aid distributed with special food coupons, everyone received a ration of fear with their ration of milk.

The municipal leaders feared threats from the mothers of their children, the mothers of all the children, should the order be given to raise a knife against the goats. From the party secretary, the mayor, on down the line, everyone was caught in a vicious circle from which they could free themselves only with difficulty. The time of the goats flowed on with its inexorable logic, more powerful than the ideology they wanted to impose by any means.

To the party strategists for municipal development it was becoming quite clear that the goatherds were moving irrevocably away from the directive sent by the central committee to turn them, at any cost, into a working class during the first five-year plan.

Ever since the goats had taken up residence in the city, the municipal party secretary had spent many sleepless nights in thought; he wanted to discover who had dreamed up the directive for the destruction of the goats: Was it the city, the republic, the federation, or the neighboring bloc of fraternal Socialist countries? He tried to figure out, from the little he had read about the history of the workers' movement and from the few books in his office, how it was possible to turn peasants, ordinary goatherds and shepherds, into a working class overnight. He could not understand why the skilled trade guilds were being closed, why those who had the knowledge of a craft passed down from generation to generation were forbidden to practice it, or why shepherds were forbidden to be shepherds—work that no one understood better than they. He could not understand any of this, and his thoughts frightened him. His innermost thoughts, thoughts he often feared he was thinking, were that someone long ago had made a mistake decreeing that the rich would become poor, and the poor, rich, overnight. And this, according to the secretary's inner thoughts, had given rise to an error that could no longer be fixed. And just as that ideology was collapsing, the goats had appeared, sent by God to correct this injustice.

The party secretary was overcome by such thoughts. But the instant he sensed he was in their thrall, he shook them off. He would summon his secretary to bring him a coffee, just so he could free himself from this line of thought. After the coffee, after he had calmed down, he consoled himself with the thought that, in any case, it was not his job to rack his brains thinking about the distant future and Communism; for this there were cleverer minds than his.

The time of the goats flowed turbulently through the city and the southern republic. The country was passing through a tangle of fateful, tragic times. The "witch hunt" continued. Trials were held; brutal theft was committed in the name of "class war"; there was no end to the religious and ideological pogroms; the evil blood of divisiveness flowed on; liquidations, silent and violent, flowed on. But through the city, fortunately, alongside the evil blood of differences, there also flowed the precious white liquid; the goat milk brought together people of different nationalities, faiths, and social origins. In these difficult times, with the wolf at the door, this goat milk became the elixir of solidarity, a formula that could not be concocted by party documents or plans for the creation of a new man.

With the goats, people in the city were closer to the roots of life. In the history of these regions, no one could recall a period of greater understanding between people and animals and of such closeness between people in this city.

One could have written a chronicle of every single family in which the goats played the most significant role. During those years, whenever anyone, a father or mother, was asked how many children he or she had, the answer would be: "Four, two boys and two goats," or "Three, two boys and one goat . . ."

With the goats' help, the cold winter days passed quickly. In that time of great tribulations, the bond between people and goats became stronger, contrary to all the expectations and desires of the party and municipal powers. After surviving the winter, no force could part them. On account of the goats, people began to call our neighborhood by the river, beside the Wooden Bridge and as far as the park, the Goatherd Quarter.

We, the children of the Goatherd Quarter, waited impatiently for the new days of spring. We waited for the river to come to life, its waters swelling from the melting snow off the mountain peaks and slopes; we waited for the willows beside the river to leaf; we waited to lead the goats to pasture.

With the coming of spring, the melting of the snows, and the rebirth of nature, people seemed braver, more assured, more enterprising, but only as far as the party would allow.

And the goats got back their vigor. They seemed to chew the very earth, to suck up every drop of its juices before they were absorbed back into the ground.

Changa dispatched a few goatherds to the party secretary with a small bucket filled with young cheese, and the party secretary contentedly nibbled it along with spring onion. Yet despite everything, the goats remained a thorn in the party's side, especially among its core cadres. They were always ready for action: roundup and slaughter.

If these cadres, these dogmatists, had known of the secret directive for transforming the goatherds into an industrial proletariat, things would not have gone well for the municipal party secretary. For now, he lived and worked in peace, in the brief calm before the inevitable storm of events, which would surely not be to his benefit.

The more measured party forces on the municipal committee had voted neither for nor against the goats. They left matters to flow on as before.

Whatever had to happen would happen!

19

One cannot avoid what is written.

"You are fatalists, dangerous fatalists," the dogmatic cadres in the committee rebuked them.

The forces wishing to take a more conciliatory tone with the goatherds and the goats were less numerous and less vocal because they feared the strident antigoat factions who were prepared to take advantage of them.

The party took no firm stand against the goats. It was becoming increasingly clear: the end of the goats would bring more harm than good, more unrest than peace. Nonetheless, as time passed, the antigoat factions became increasingly persistent. They sought meetings open to the public where the choice would be clear: the goats or the party.

The party secretary became increasingly worried by these demands; at one meeting someone even called for his dismissal, and on occasion he did consider leaving his job. But he quickly chased the thought away. Because were he to leave and a new secretary selected, as soon as he opened the strongbox, he would discover the secret directive and put it into effect, citing the obvious aggressiveness of the goats and so advance his career . . . As for him, the recent leading figure in the city, things would end badly. Still, many times he opened the strongbox, read the directive for the hundredth time, and then fingered his pistol. The directive seemed to lead him unconsciously to the pistol. Eventually, he concluded that it would be best not to open the strongbox, nor did he give anyone else occasion to.

Meanwhile, the nannies—a plague upon them—ran wild that spring. In a flurry, they gamboled unattended through the city like white phantoms—often whole herds of them. Especially when they were on the prowl for Changa's bucks.

The goats had to pass the offices of the municipal committee of the party, just below the secretary's window. The secretary closed the windows; he saw nothing, heard nothing. He thought he heard whispered comments: in the not-too-distant future the goatherds would overwhelm the city with their goats; the day of the white goat counterrevolution was not far off, when a goatherd with his goatskin partisan's cap would occupy the secretary's chair.

Complaints from the central organizations of the party began to reach the municipal committee concerning the goats' indecent behavior in public places.

There was even a complaint from the party committee at the theater. Goatherds were said to be arriving at performances accompanied by a goat or two. In reality, it was the children, but those children had parents! Once a goat had even ambled onto the stage during a performance of *Carmen*! Fortunately, the goat had merely walked across the stage. The audience did not even notice; they thought that a goat appeared in the scene. But no one from the opera could silence the scandal. So another complaint reached the municipal secretary. Complaints were coming from all sides. The goats were entering the movie theaters, stores, pharmacies, and markets. All eyes were turned to the party secretary. He wisely kept his mouth shut. He knew that no one was ready for the decisive step; everyone was dependent on the goats, bewitched by them. He could find some comfort there.

3

*W*e lived in the heart of the Goatherd Quarter by the river in an old two-story house, one in a row of houses built in Ottoman architectural styles from the turn of the twentieth century blended with an obvious admixture of European elements.

The house had a long courtyard leading to a spacious garden surrounded by the walls of the neighboring houses.

Life by the rapid river created the illusion of constant motion. Our new house appealed greatly to Father's Odyssean spirit.

Once we had been uprooted from our native soil, the river constantly beckoned us to continue our migration farther, to unknown territories, out toward the sea. When life was difficult, the river suggested other possibilities, but we remained here forever.

My father was fortunate that the house had wide and deep cabinets that he could fill with the old documents, books, maps, and manuscripts he had rescued during our various resettlements, wars, fires, and floods. He came to this unknown city with only a pile of books and a family of many children, leaving behind his native hearth and kin on the shores of a wondrous lake.

Life by the river provided some comfort for the lost lake, but our migrations were always uncertain, cursed; they took away some things and brought others. This was how the circle of fate was fulfilled for this uprooted Balkan family. My father's books brought him the greatest comfort during the meanderings of his fate. Yes, he had rescued them from wars and misfortunes, and they, in turn, had shown him the path to safety during other times, which, though peaceful, were filled with uncertainty. His books widened the family circle.

Books and reading gave us strength in our battles with time. When crucial family decisions had to be made, my father turned to his books. The books held my father back from precipitous decisions in his life.

In the cabinets of the new house, he kept every imaginable kind of book, both sacred and scholarly, written in Arabic, Latin, or Cyrillic script. He had old encyclopedias, books relating to astronomy, history, law, and the history of religions, dictionaries, grammars, maps, and atlases.

We were hemmed in, confined within ever-changing and uncertain Balkan borders, but the books broadened our horizons and carried us long distances. My father's books held a mysterious bond with the harmony and happiness of our family. Father often collected books he could depend on along our uncertain path.

In her fashion, my mother, poor thing, shared Father's love of books; it was a part of their long-lasting and quiet love. During our migrations, it was with a heavy heart that she would leave behind some object used in her housekeeping. For example, she could never quite forgive herself for having left behind, on account of several of Father's books, the hand-cranked pasta machine she had bought during the only trip she ever took to Italy. But she believed there was hidden in Father's books, perhaps precisely in those very books, something more sacred, more fateful for the destiny of the family, than in the only such pasta machine in the city.

Father's books became sacred to my mother, and she passed that love to us.

Sometimes during migrations and times of war we marched along the trenches carrying books instead of blanket, pillow, or bag. But after we had settled into our house by the rapid river, tormented by hunger in these postwar years, my father—left without family and those close friends with whom one easily shares the last crust of bread—fell into constant reading of his books. More and more he resembled a Balkan Don Quixote, unable to find a way out for his family on whose doors hunger was rapping with increasing persistence.

My mother could not understand why, even here in this country where the family had to put down roots and build a life with others, my father stayed up late at night with his books.

When she slipped into his study, unnoticed, to bring him tea or something she had prepared for the children, there on the table she would see books spread wide open—encyclopedias or atlases of astronomy, zoology, and botany.

She saw gigantic butterflies, stars, and goats in the illustrations and could not understand what problem my father was tracking down at a time when there was not enough to feed their children. Her soul ached when we went to bed hungry or when, instead of dinner, we doled out roasted chickpeas one by one. My mother and father would be left without even the chickpeas. Yet all through the night, my father would continue to think, leaf through his books, read. Often, the first rays of sunlight would extinguish the lamp shining through the night above my father's books.

Mother recalled one such night in their old house by the lake when Father had discovered in his oldest Constantinople document— handwritten in Arabic script—where nearby chrome ore deposits were located. He tried to pass this information on to those in power locally and then to the ministers, then to the head of state. He wrote, sent letters, but no one called him or asked to meet with him. Our mother told us later that, just as my father's notes described, these very locations were explored, and chrome was unearthed. Veins of chrome were discovered leading toward the bowels of the mountain, where one could mine for centuries. My mother said that some shrewd people came, excavated, and got rich; my father continued into the future with his books.

My mother never spoke about this while Father was alive. But at that time of hunger, when for the first time death knocked on the doors of our family home, when she saw my father engrossed in his books, she feared that something like what had happened with the chrome ore would happen again. My father discovered things, but others enjoyed the fruits of his labor. Death, with tragic consequences for our family, now frightened her. My father maintained an enigmatic silence as he patiently calmed her with the tranquility of his blue eyes, which always radiated hope. His patience, this quiet hope, would be transferred to my mother, and she passed it on to us. We interpreted the messages she brought us from Father's study in different ways. When one of us woke during the night, frightened by a dream or tormented by hunger, we would all lie awake, waiting for the dawn, hoping she would bring us bread. This feeling of hope was strengthened by the ever-shining glow from Father's golden lamp. This golden light remained forever with us, that light above his books shining as he searched for an exit when life turned difficult.

My father clearly sensed that hunger, nearly chronic hunger, was withering our souls; he felt our vitality draining, and it, in turn, drained his enthusiasm for reading and contemplation.

Mother used what little flour we had to mix a dough—something ordinary, different forms of noodles and pitas, but always with a new twist—to quell our hunger. She could make us believe we were eating something new every day when, in fact, it was always the same dough! But when my father brought home a tomato, or my mother waited for something to ripen in her garden, then the color of our daily dough changed. It would be bright red; then, stretched, it would turn a paler red, become a festive dinner so tasty you would lick your fingers. My father well knew, and my mother needed no convincing: our bodies needed milk, more milk, and still more milk for us to be strong, for our bones to grow straight, for our lives to begin on the right track.

☆

My father, a graduate of the University of Constantinople, had left behind a career in the upper echelons of the new Turkish administration; he had been recommended by Atatürk himself after a meeting with him (which he never spoke about, especially during the Stalin era); he was an authority on Ottoman script. He discovered texts tracing the history of the Balkan nations through three centuries, and through them he rescued his family. A leading authority of both sharia and modern European law, my father felt a kind of atavistic pull toward his internal Balkan center of gravity but could not free himself of his Odyssean spirit when the waves of fate cast him here beside the river in this city, where once again he had to prove to himself that he could resettle his uprooted family, now facing hunger, true hunger, for the first time. Hungry, worried about his family, with a civil servant's pay barely enough to make it through the end of the month, my father tried, using all the learning he had acquired and his library of Eastern and Western books, to understand the creeds of this new era that people swore by— Socialism and Communism.

He was well acquainted with these ideas from Western sources, but he could not connect them with the hunger and the chronic poverty of these people with no factories, railways, collectives, people who had never been as hungry as they were now.

He feared that this "ideology" had been mistakenly adopted from books and even more mistakenly transplanted here and put into practice. He feared this most, and here he was closest to the truth.

In his frequent musings, he concluded that the Balkans most often suffered from their adoption of mistaken "ideologies" but were also victims of ideologies imposed by others, more powerful conquerors and empires. Now, however, was not the time to delve into these mistaken ideas; he had to find a way out for his family, a way out of hunger.

In moments of crystalline solitude in the heart of the Balkan night, when he easily slipped into his subconscious thoughts, he reflected that the situation in which his family found itself was perhaps fate's revenge. When it had offered him the brightest destiny, he had rejected it. His conflict with the Ottoman Empire had a deep genesis. He feared other circles of Janissary hell, invisible ones. There were many books in his library dedicated to the Janissaries, on whom the rise and fall of the Ottoman Empire depended. He always maintained that even if the Balkan empires had disappeared, the Janissary spirit that had maintained them had not. He was afraid, at least for himself and for his family, of becoming a slave to that spirit.

My father feared that the contradictions of the Ottoman Empire — which he knew and understood so well — would continue into the new era, the era of Socialism and Communism, under the guise of totalitarianism.

He feared that someone would sow the Janissary ideology in new form among his beloved Balkan peoples.

My father's life in the Balkans covered three-quarters of the twentieth century. He often stood face to face with key events in its history. He thought it good for a person to flow with the course of history, but he himself did the opposite. He remained forever convinced that history was written only by the victors, who feared revenge and defeat.

My father would say that he believed in the history of the truth. But it had not yet been written. Someone had to write it. Until the discovery of that history of truth, according to my father, one had to read books of all times. He devoted his life to this.

And so in his conflict with history, he threw his life onto the bank of this river to live with people who would be victims of this new "Janissary ideology" — the ideology of Communism. He understood Communism, like all other ideologies, to be a mere facade of real life.

My father was firmly convinced that one ideology — better yet, a single faith — was sufficient for a person, for humanity. If there were two faiths, if Communism were superimposed on religion, there would be unnecessary and destructive conflicts among people. He feared that the consequences of this double allegiance, this "Janissary spirit," would, in the Balkans, be more violent than history had known in other parts of the world.

When he thought about the future of his descendants in the Balkans, he most feared the violence resulting from allegiance to multiple ideologies. As proof of his thesis he took the Communists' bloody settling of accounts with the religious leaders of nearly every faith. He considered the idea of founding museums of atheism an abomination. He feared that the settling of accounts with religious leaders would be more violent and more persistent and would leave more serious consequences in the most backward regions of the Balkans, and this covered almost all its territory. He respected those states in which religion was kept separate from the state and from ideology in the most peaceful way possible.

It was not easy for my father to make sense of this time of the goats, to enter it and submit to it. He thought that the banal question—whether to ban goats in the first years of Communism—had become a true test, a first obstacle on which Communism had stumbled, and from that moment it began its collapse due to its powerlessness to engage for long with the reality of the way life was truly lived . . .

Unlike my father, Mother did not contemplate the weight of history theoretically. For my mother, history was us—her hungry children with no goats, and all the well-fed children in those families with goats.

4

$\mathcal{M}$y mother rarely, quite rarely, went into my father's study late at night when he was poring over his open books. You could count the times on your fingers. When she did, my father was certain that something big was weighing on her soul.

At those moments, as he looked with concern in her face, he was certain that she had been busy trying to solve a problem, most often one tormenting the entire family, and now the time had come for its resolution.

Fateful family decisions took a long time to mature in my parents' souls. When the time came, their thoughts flowed into one and merged. There was never haste from one side or the other.

My mother entered the room silently. My father recognized her shadow playing among his books. He lifted his head from the opened books and, with his eternally gentle expression, caught my mother's worried look.

"Forgive me for bothering you," my mother began immediately. "I had to. I am so sorry to say this, but the children have gone to bed without so much as a crust of bread; they are hungry. We don't have a speck of flour."

As she spoke, my father turned his thoughts from his books; he took off his glasses and gathered his strength to soothe my mother. He could not remember seeing her in such a state. He said, "I was promised a sack of flour tomorrow. We can hold out until the coupons and my pay next month . . ."

"The children are tired of pitas and noodles made of nothing but flour and water. Our children, it pains me to say, have not tasted milk for months," my mother continued with concern.

It was immediately clear to my father that she was thinking about the goats, the neighbor's goats, the goats of all the families in the Goatherd Quarter . . . He did not say a word. His silence was more powerful than any answer. They always understood each other through their silences.

The sharp and uneven breathing of the sleeping children cut the quiet of the night, and from time to time, the bleating of the goats from the nearby neighbors could be heard.

My father did not say a word; he looked her gently in the eye. Several tears played at the corners of her eyes, tears my father sensed before they formed.

As a rule, my mother interrupted his nighttime reading and contemplation only when she had something of critical importance to tell him. Surely she had not come to tell him that the children were hungry. This was nothing new. She would interrupt when she sensed death knocking on our family's doorstep, ready to carry off one of their worn-out children. But this time my mother had come to tell him about the new child she was carrying in her tortured womb.

Poor families are always lucky or unlucky in the same way. They seem to have equal capacity for suffering and good fortune. It had been difficult for my father to become accustomed to these revolutionary times when generations upon generations had to be uprooted and start again from the beginning.

My father, in a different, more profound way, had been fully absorbed by these cursed times when people believed more in salvation by goats than in salvation by revolutionary changes. He shared my mother's pain of knowing that they could not give their children enough to eat, but he tried to understand the root of the problem and sought possible paths of escape. We children knew why Mother intended to go to Father's room, and we waited to hear the result, but in the meantime, we went to our closest neighbors to enjoy their goats. We were often given a glass of milk or a piece of bread with clotted cream made from goat milk.

Our family's calendar followed a cycle of births and deaths. Everything was so intermingled in those cursed times. Time and again, Mother gave birth to a child to take the place of one that had died. This is how she maintained the life of the family; it was in these hungry years that she was most exhausted. This new pregnancy caught my father in the most difficult circumstance of his life. What would this new birth mean to the blackness of their poverty, when all that remained was the family's long-abiding hope? As usual in the Balkans, everything was again uncertain during this hellish time, in this troubled half-century marked by the fall of two powerful empires, two world wars that took place even before the memory of the Balkan wars had faded. There was too much tragic history—with its unavoidable migrations and clashes of life and death—to skip past a single family.

My father fell into deep thought. The golden lamp glowing amid my father's books shone for nights on end. My mother, pressed by the weight of the unborn child and the hunger of her other children, gazed long into the night at the sad beams of Father's lamp without the truth being illuminated to her.

My father followed the steady flow of his thoughts. The decision was simple: like everyone else, he had to buy a goat. My mother's presence forced him to think about the goats not only philosophically but as something absolutely concrete and real, as real as life itself.

As she left his study, my mother quietly slipped onto the table the last gold napoleon she had received from her father-in-law, who had died long ago; it was to be kept and used only in a time of great calamity. Once, in his younger years, my father had saved his head with one of those napoleons when a foreign soldier had locked him up following an altercation with the new occupying regime.

My grandfather had then begged my mother to guard this gold piece like a hawk. Everything in life passes quickly . . . My mother felt that the time had come, because hunger was threatening to destroy the family. The gold coin sparkled in the glow of Father's lamp. The message was clear.

Now my father began to consider in concrete and realistic terms how to go about buying a goat.

That is what my mother had decreed.

That is what fate had decreed.

My father, a nonparty member, knew that if he bought a goat, he would be first in the line of fire should the government impose a strict ban against keeping goats. As for the ban, there were already whispers from the government. But he knew himself quite well: having once set out along the goatherds' path, he would fully devote himself to them, would lead them, would show them his books about goats, and would truly embrace the time of the goats. Henceforth, he was less afraid of the goats than he was of himself. He knew that the people would not reconcile themselves to a ban against goats; they would openly revolt, they would oppose it, and they would fight. He would be among the first to engage in that war.

My father was a newcomer, a foreigner in this city, not a migrant like the goatherds. He was an immigrant, a person who had crossed the border; he had to show his allegiance and withhold his criticism so that one day he and his family could receive their sought-after citizenship, confirmation of their loyalty to this new country.

The purchase of a goat put him between two evils. He must choose the lesser one, but he did not know which that was.

5

One morning, my father left the house unusually early, as if he were being led by one of those bright thoughts that he had at the border between night and day.

We were surprised that he did not take with him the black, weathered briefcase he always carried when he went to work.

My mother, exhausted from the impending birth, took note of Father's departure, but she could not stand up to see him to the door as she always did in their life together, to give him her gentle smile, a quiet expression of hope for his safe return. In their youth, this send-off had been a small ritual completed with the tender touch of their lips; now, with that same love, it was the touch of their glances.

That afternoon, while we children were engrossed in our games outside, my mother collected her final strength and, from the flour my father had brought, tried some new sorcery to prepare us something for lunch, different from yesterday's; her fingers playfully mixed the same old dough as if they held none of her body's fatigue.

We children, especially the younger ones, who grew hungry sooner, frequently went into the kitchen to see what new things Mother was making. Most of the time, the reason we went in was to check on how she was feeling after having taken a long morning rest because of her pains rather than to check on our lunch. We all felt the same way. And when we saw our mother's lively fingers winding the dough into unimaginable forms, we forgot our hunger and set off, heartened, back into the yard.

It was the same this last time, but as we were going down the long hallway connecting the kitchen with the courtyard, we clearly heard from the doorway a bleating sound entering our kitchen. We told ourselves that it must be one of the neighbor's goats wandering into the wrong door by mistake. But we already knew the sound of their bleating. This was a different voice. The little goat met us in the courtyard. And here was Father walking behind her.

"May this little goat bring you happiness!" my father called out happily.

"Daddy's bought a goat, Daddy's bought a goat!" we all screamed together, loud enough to be heard by our mother, our neighbors, the other goats, the whole of the Goatherd Quarter, the city, the party, the country, the entire Balkan Peninsula . . .

In the childhood of poor families, there is always one moment, long desired and anticipated, when the door of fate—which must lead to a different future—opens. For us children and for our family, the goat my father had bought pushed open that little door, and, together with our goat, we stepped surely and irrevocably into the time of the goats.

Childhood often mingles with paradise. With our little goat we were there. Our minds still held the lasting memories, images, of our first and last family voyage, when, as if aboard Noah's ark, we crossed the border in an old rowboat bought from one of my father's trusted friends. We abandoned our first childhood paradise without understanding Father's reasons for our sudden departure.

The old rowboat traversing the moonlit lake stayed in our memory as large as a sea, expanding through time to the size of an ocean. In the restlessness of the waves we forever lost our native shore, which could never be erased from our memories.

This goat now connected us with our lost paradise. Fragments of a large family torn apart and carried across to this other shore, we had to find a new home, new friends to replace those relatives, our nearest kin, who were lost. After we had suffered so much adjusting to this new land on life's new shore, here was this goat to help us replace what had been lost, the missing parts of our childhood. Because of the little kid my father bought on that bright day in our family's history, the goats became our first close kin.

The little goat had to bring us closer to all the other people, to all the other nationalities in this country. We welcomed our kid as we did Mother's newborns. We had one more reason to fear the future: it held not only the fear of our parents' death but the death of our goat as well.

The bleating of the goat reached all the corners of our house before they would hear the cries of the baby Mother was expecting. Mother was busy in the kitchen and had no idea what was going on in the courtyard. With her last bit of strength, she dragged herself outside to join in our happiness. She looked at our father with eyes filled with the tenderness of her feelings and thoughts but also with a shadow of concern, that the day might come when there would be other need for the gold piece. But our childish joy was stronger than everything else. Poor families are nearly all alike: they are happy or unhappy in the same way. But one thing is certain: the wealth of poor families is their children and life itself. Here in our new country, our parents had only us and we had only them, but now—we also had our little goat.

"Daddy bought us a goat!" All of us hugged our mother as we brought the goat closer.

Mother embraced us in her happiness. Our happiness gave meaning to her life, and this new joy was now a part of this happiness.

This is how the most significant time of our childhood unfolded. Here in our midst, bleating happily, was our little doe, her white hair and shaggy golden forehead shining like the rays of the sun.

"We have a golden goat!" I shouted.

"It is golden, it is a golden goat!" everyone else chimed in.

The news that my father had bought a goat quickly spread through the Goatherd Quarter. First to come were our closest neighbors' children. And our joy became theirs.

The news reached the city as well. Goatherds whom we knew, and some we did not, arrived to congratulate my father on his purchase.

"Bravo, congratulations, neighbors, you are now one of us. With you and your goat with us, we will be stronger!"

My father had simply been tossed by the waves of fate into what was now known as the Goatherd Quarter, into this dilapidated house by the river, shaded by the row of towering poplars planted during the Ottoman era; it was difficult for him to adapt to life in this time of the goats. With his black-trimmed gray hat—a hat he had started to wear back in the 1920s when he was still a student in Constantinople living with some of his close maternal relatives, a hat that remained with him to the end of his life—and his black briefcase overflowing with books and old Ottoman documents, he had remained somehow apart from these people who were caught up in their lives. He needed to take just one step, the fateful step to buy a goat, to step into the parade of life around him. He found himself joined with people who never read, many of whom had never seen a book in their lives, particularly those who had come down from the higher mountains with their big, healthy goats. Yet these people looked with great pity at my father, who dragged his black briefcase of books every day but could not feed his starving children. They felt sorry that he was in no position to buy the most ordinary of goats to save his family! There were others, however, cleverer ones for whom the goats had obviously changed the course of their lives for the better, those for whom the goats had brought material security and peace into their homes, who had reasons, other reasons, to see my father with a goat.

There were all kinds of theories as to why my father would, or would not, buy a goat. Some people spread a rumor through the Goatherd Quarter and across the city that my father had been housed in the Goatherd Quarter by the government, allegedly in order to remain in secret communication with the party, to keep track of ties between goats and people. There was a time when people simply could not reconcile his family's hunger with his stubborn refusal to buy a goat, as all normal people did for their children. They concluded that he was a true party zealot, prepared to watch his children die rather than deviate from party policy concerning the goat question. There were other voices saying that my father was connected with foreign intelligence services, even three at once! There were other, contradictory, rumors calling my father a fanatical opponent of Socialism and Communism, a class enemy who did not want to show solidarity with this new class supported by the goatherds. Some of these rumors reached our ears, but the most important thing for us was this: Father had bought a goat, and Mother was happy with all her children. The rumors soon quieted down. My father gradually became an authority among the goatherds. At last, we were accepted members of the Goatherd Quarter.

6

*B*efore buying the goat, Father thought long and hard about the consequences of the "class struggle" in the Balkans. He could not understand how the idea had been transplanted from the French and October Revolutions to the Balkans, where it survived in corrupted forms and took many lives. In the name of "class struggle," man had never been so debased.

My father was nearing the conclusion that here in the Balkans, goats ameliorated the consequences of the terrible class struggle. The Communist strategists, under the cloak of Stalinism, thought the same but did not say so publicly: "The goats can incite counterrevolution in the defeated class!" There was a danger, according to their supporters, of the goats bringing together "opposing classes": the craftsmen and the workers, the self-employed and the civil servants, the believers and the Communists, the defeated and the victors. Some secret party documents even wrote of the danger—were immediate action not taken—that the cry "Proletariats of the world unite!" would become "Goatherds of the world unite!" My father considered the idea that after its victory over Fascism, the party—following the old model of the French Revolution, adopted and impoverished by the protagonists of the October Revolution—must take into account the five centuries of Ottoman rule, as a result of which class warfare in the Balkans would be radically different. He was clearly afraid that the day was not far off when the goatherds themselves would unknowingly get mixed up in the cursed "class struggle." He was not sure when it would happen, but it was clear to him that the party had specified a D-day for the final indictment and liquidation of the goats.

In carefully chosen words, my father tried to explain all this to my mother to delay purchasing a goat. But she, poor thing, with her un-failing instinct to protect the lives of her children, told him in plain language that their children might all be dead by D-day. Better to have the children alive until then and the goats dead afterward. My father silently accepted the logic of this argument, which was perhaps decisive in his decision to buy the goat, and set his black thoughts aside for the future.

He had a deep and intuitive understanding of the goatherds with whom—with his purchase of a goat—he had tied his fate and that of his family. The goatherds had been uprooted from their hearths in the mountains, just as we had been uprooted from our native lakeside home. Of course, the motives were different, but we were all refugees in this city, equally tormented by history.

The party had promised a radiant future to all these people if they would just come down from the mountains and become the new working class—strong, steely, fervent, fearless, invincible—to strike the fatal blow against the last remnants of the vanquished class. They had to become this new class! That was the order; that was the plan. According to my father, the goatherds, after rescuing themselves from the large village collectives, having come down from the mountains, now found themselves in a trap. It was difficult, if not impossible, for the new regime to turn these people, overnight, into their imagined working class.

These were difficult postwar times. Fascism had been defeated. Communism had declared a new era. The Berlin Wall divided Europe.

The Iron Curtain had descended. Stalinism had already, through its prewar pact with Hitler, compromised the future of Communism. The naive continued to believe in miracles. Despite the death camps, deportations, and gulags, a belief in Soviet Communism was maintained in the Balkans. Here, with its chronic delay and with more acute consequences, the complex of contradictions, from which Europe had already recovered, was unfolding. A Berlin Wall had risen between people. Stalin, first discreetly and later openly, began to threaten the recalcitrant Balkan peoples with his schemes of conquest. Therefore, the Balkan strategists had to wait for calmer times to transform millions of goatherds into the working class and to liquidate the goats; until then, the goatherds and the goats must be under the watchful eye of the federal Communist Party.

In his wide-ranging thoughts on the goat question, Father was convinced that the regime had developed a number of strategies for an end to the goats in each separate Yugoslav republic, depending on the level of development and mentality of its people.

My father suspected that the party and the government had established special task forces to delve deeply into the reasons for this bond between goats and the peoples of the Balkans. Particular attention was given to the development of reports damning the goats. Every possible fact on this topic was documented. Through secret channels, foreign literature was acquired, libraries were consulted, well-known examples citing the dangers of goats were assembled. Books dealing with the positive aspects of goats were willfully ignored. My father was fixated on this idea as he tried to find other literature, books in praise of goats. After all, in his library he had earlier acquired many such books about goats, long before any question about them had arisen. From my father's books one could compile quite a history of goats and goat herding in the Balkans, the Mediterranean, and Europe.

My father had books that contained wide-ranging discussions of questions relating to how goats had depleted the forests of Spain, Sicily, Corsica, the valley in the Atlas Mountains of North Africa, all the way to the Black Sea. He had books concerned with the great divide at the beginning of the century between those European nations for, and those against, goats. The nations in favor of goats had put forth clear arguments contradicting claims made by the antigoat factions about the harm goats caused: goats had discovered coffee and had demonstrated that by cutting the vines, more grapes were produced; if one compares the weight of goats and cows, goats give eight to ten times more milk per pound than cows do. The most significant discovery my father found in his books was the scientific proof that the casein of goat milk is particularly easy to digest because of the light and delicate nature of its curd, which is similar to mother's milk. My father gleaned these facts from a rare book, perhaps the sole copy in the Balkans. The fact that goat milk resembles mother's milk pleased him. This was perhaps his strongest argument in the battle with the antigoat factions. But to whom could he make this argument? Despite all the benefits goats offered humans, especially the poor, saving them from hunger, illness, and death, despite the many reasons it should be considered the best domestic animal, for many people, goats remained the most underrated animal. In many countries, the rich looked with contempt on this "Balkan cow," the cow of the poor.

There were many, many secrets in Father's books about goats. But no one in the family, and fewer in the Goatherd Quarter, knew of those books about goats. My father seemed to have books about all the difficult times in the Balkans. And this was one of them, the time of the goats.

7

*T*he goat quickly changed life for our family as well. Not a day passed without my father learning something new about goats and their owners. For years, the neighbors had looked suspiciously at the only man in the neighborhood to wear a hat, the man who left the house every day at the same time with his black bag and returned late at night. Now my father had become a completely different person to these people. He was theirs. They often came to our house; they were enchanted and cheered by their conversations with him about goats. They became Father's new friends.

One morning, the lead goatherd, Changa, a living legend during the time of the goats, came to visit my father accompanied by several other well-known goatherds. Changa was a tall, strapping man with long blond hair, an eagle nose, a solid face with ruddy cheeks, and a broad forehead. Although illiterate, he was a smart and brave man. Had it not been for Changa, the goats would surely have been left on the road halfway to the city during our first winter of freedom. He had a whole herd of select Saanen does and several shaggy bucks, used for stud each spring, when masses of goats in season were brought to them.

Changa was not a party member, so conversation with my father was easygoing. Their characters seemed to complement each other, and they quickly grew close. They became good friends, inseparable. We children learned that Changa was just his nickname; his real name was Melko Melovski. The goat question brought my father and Changa together. The lead goatherd began to come to our house often, which noticeably increased our family's reputation among the goatherds in the Goatherd Quarter and more widely throughout the city, even though we had only one tender goat, a goat golden to us children.

Changa walked with a heavy, firm tread. When we heard the creak of the stairs leading to Father's room, we knew that Changa was coming. We would go into Father's room so we could see Changa and say hello to him, and he would often give us a coin or two. Then, happy, we would go into the neighborhood with our goat to announce who had come to our house. Everyone listened to us with enthusiasm.

We never fully understood what my father and Changa talked about, but we knew that part of the conversation was always about goats and our future with them.

Changa sometimes stayed with my father and his books until dawn. Father would read to him, explaining things from the wide-open books, some with illustrations of goats. Changa listened, enraptured. He looked at the pictures. He was particularly struck by an old lithograph in which one could clearly see a Saanen goat suckling a lion. "Is it really possible," he asked my father dubiously, "for a goat to suckle a lion?!" "Yes, it's possible, it's possible," my father assured him.

For the first time, Changa grew sad. He truly regretted that he did not know how to read; he regretted that he was illiterate, uneducated to his very soul. He begged Father to help him become literate, to teach him to read. And so, while Father read the books to Changa about goats, he taught him to read. With his quick and natural intelligence, Changa easily learned "the little letters," as he told my father in jest. After his long conversation with my father, we watched him leave with a book or two, perhaps some notes. Later, through his connections in the Balkans and beyond, Changa brought my father new books about goats, and together they read them and discussed them.

From Father's books, Changa learned that the goat was the first animal whose milk humans drank. Our house had somehow become the first goat university in the Balkans, whose sole student was Changa and then, through him, all the goatherds. As a sign of thanks, he wanted to give us a goat. My father did not want to accept one at any price. Changa was adamant; for the first time in his life, he was begging someone to do something, and in the end, my father, looking at his children, accepted. It was as though a holiday had suddenly descended on our house. We had received a goat from Changa, the great goatherd. He said that because of Father's good deeds, our family was helping the entire herd; we were helping all the goats and people in the city.

Changa certainly learned quite a bit about goats from the books, but my father learned quite a bit about life from Changa, especially about the nature of goats. After my father had developed complete trust in Changa, he began to tell him his fears concerning the goats and the "unfinished class struggle," as stated in the large banners posted throughout the city. When Father was with Changa, his soul opened so wide that fear, like a bird, flew away.

The goatherd was fearless. He had been raised with goats, but he knew people even better. In the city, there was not a single person with a goat, party member or not, who did not use the services of Changa's bucks to impregnate their goats. That wasn't all. With his expansive, noble soul, Changa was first to help the hungry and the poor in the city: he brought milk and food and was prepared to give one of his goats' newborn kids to the poorest among them. And his goats were fertile, very fertile.

And so Changa's herd—with all the kids born to does impregnated by his bucks—spread throughout the whole city and the entire republic. Changa even entered the houses of party leaders, government representatives, and the army. Although they protested that they either did not want or were unable in principle to keep goats, their children and families could not survive without the goat milk. Secretly, through his faithful goatherds, Changa sent milk and cheese to these functionaries and as a result he had "nearly everyone in his pocket," as he once joked to my father.

Yoo, in the course of not quite a year, Changa learned to read well The following year, he began to borrow books more often from Father's library, not only books about goats but others as well. Now their conversations were not centered on goats alone.

My father told Changa about his life. For a long time, his life and the history of our family had been kept secret from everyone in the Goatherd Quarter and in the city. Our family—newcomers with a different language and faith (yet subjected to the same ideology), with its unusual collection of books, cast up by the river in this city during the time of the goats—had for a long time been like an unreachable island.

With great enthusiasm, my father continued his work involving the translation of old Ottoman-era documents, written between the sixteenth and nineteenth centuries, documents of significance to everyone in this part of the Balkans, documents he himself had discovered on one of his many quests.

One evening, he confided in Changa how his writing about goats and research on many facets of their symbiotic life with humans were connected to one of his life projects, a history of the Balkan empires, in which goats played a role. He wanted to bring together his thoughts about goats with the knowledge he had gathered about the Janissaries, the ever-present echelon in all the Balkan empires, always present but under different names. Through the fate of the Janissaries he wanted to learn about all the other conquerors of the Balkans.

Changa listened to him intently, even though he lacked much of the knowledge and concepts one needed in order to understand all this completely. But as soon as my father mentioned goats, he would strain his attention to understand what he was hearing. When Father finished his explanation about this unusual combination, Changa could only exclaim, "I just can't understand the relationship between the goats and the Janissaries!"

My father was surprised by Changa's question, posed so intelligently and in the spirit of my father's main ideas. He often forgot that here before him was a man who had just recently learned to read and that he needed to be selective in the concepts he discussed. But Changa had a razor-sharp mind. The right words attached themselves to his soul; he had long ago learned the alphabet of ideas, of life, and now knowledge of script simply helped his lucid thoughts move more quickly. Changa, incidentally, knew by heart hundreds of songs, sayings, and stories.

My father looked at him thoughtfully for a long time before he answered him: "It is difficult to say when goats first appeared in the Balkans, and it is even more difficult to determine whether they were autochthonous, that is to say, native."

My father began to explain the word *autochthonous* more broadly, and he continued: "In a certain German book, it states that the goat appeared in Europe during the time of the barbarian invasions. This is perhaps when the European prejudice against the Balkans was born. Though who can ascertain who were the barbarians and who the civilized autochthonous people? Because of the Balkans' accursed history, there is still no end to the settling of accounts between empires and nations; there is still no end to divisions. Most often, it was the absent Balkan people who were deemed guilty, because everyone hurled condemnation farthest from themselves, off toward the distant Balkans, where else?"

Changa listened more attentively than ever. His shadow, from time to time, flickered in the rays of the lamp above Father's books.

"But in other books," my father continued, "I have read how goats have lived with people since as early as the time of the so-called pile dwellings, the oldest human houses."

Changa, ever since he had learned so quickly to read, carried a yellow notebook in which he was always jotting things down. My father waited for him to finish writing, and then he continued: "I owe you an answer to the question about the connection between the goats and the Janissaries. At a glance, it would seem that there is no special connection. But the goats are a kind of 'Janissary' among domestic animals. The goats in many ways betrayed their wild ancestors and grew close to people."

"That's right!" cried out Changa with satisfaction.

"But I was thinking about something else. All the 'barbarians' who came to the Balkans across the sea, across rivers and dry land, had powerful military organizations. They were conquerors of vast territories. All wanted the Balkans to be the last stage of their great campaigns of conquest. The Romans, for example, were the bearers of a great and strong civilization. They entered the Balkans with a strategy: divide and conquer! After them came the Byzantines. They carried the Roman strategy further. The divisions continued, differences continued, they splintered the diverse groups of people. Then the Ottomans arrived. They fortified themselves in our city to remain here for centuries and then continued on to Europe, stopping at the gates of Vienna. They remained in the Balkans more than five centuries. Up to our own century. And they inherited the old formula: divide and conquer. They had learned enough from the earlier European empires, and they did not ignore the experiences of their Asiatic-Persian ancestors. What have the Balkans not endured?

"They opened new divisions, based mainly on faith, and so new Janissaries were created. They would raise the empire to its highest point but cause its downfall as well. In the name of the law, the blood tax—the so-called *devshirme*, or 'selection'—children were estranged from their families, torn from their fathers, mothers, brothers, and sisters, all their kin when they were still young, just twelve to fifteen years of age. In special military academies in Constantinople, they were taught the arts of war. When they completed their study, they were placed into the elite military units as Janissaries. The Janissaries were recruited from nearly all the Balkan peoples: Serbs, Albanians, Macedonians, Montenegrins, Bulgarians . . ."

Changa could not figure out where my father was going, but he closely followed the link between the goats and the Balkan Janissaries, and he said, more to himself, "And during all these hard times in the Balkans, were the goats always with people?"

"Yes," my father acknowledged, "the goats were with the people in all these difficult times, not just here but more broadly in the lands of the Mediterranean, the Balkans, even as distant as the Far East. It was the goat 'Janissaries' that saved people from the Janissaries created by the great empires. This conflict did not stop in the Balkans. The goats remained on the side of the poor, the dependent, the abandoned, the outsiders . . ."

"So that's where the Balkan saying comes from: 'Death to your neighbor's goat!'" cried Changa, pleased with himself.

"One could say that," my father granted. "The saying can be considered the people's response to the imperial slogan, 'Divide and conquer!' But we can't be sure exactly during which empire the expression arose."

A long silence ensued.

The two were looking through a number of books. Changa was first to raise his eyes and turn to the picture of the goat suckling the lion. He often asked my father if it were really possible for a goat to suckle a lion cub or whether the artist had simply dreamed this up. My father, after he had introduced Changa to the existence of myths, tried to give a more complete answer: "The mythic legend portrays the she-goat as a divine emissary who, in the form of the gracious beauty Almathea, would suckle the baby Jupiter, as the god Zeus was later called by the Romans."

"Who was Zeus?" asked Changa.

"Zeus, or Jupiter, was the greatest of the gods, god of the heavens, of light and thunder."

Changa had to ask my father why he was mixing up the planet Jupiter with a god. Then he recalled the many old legends dedicated to goats told in his native region. Comparing them, he discovered new things. In those legends, too, the goat became a divine emissary and protector of the poor.

8

Changa felt elated when he left our house late at night, sometimes just before dawn, books tucked under his arm.

Happy, he rushed to his goats, played with them, milked them, and got them ready for pasture. While they grazed, he read to the goatherds from Father's books. The goatherds listened attentively, though from time to time they would tilt their heads, doubtful and simply unable to believe what was in the books.

After all, how was it possible for these goats, now peacefully grazing, to be so mixed up in the history of mankind and the planet? They doubted even more something Changa swore was true: goats nursed lion cubs.

The news spread quickly through the city that Changa read to the goatherds while grazing his goats. Changa was not just anybody. His movements were followed vigilantly by the police, his words by the party, and his goats by the government. Changa inflicted unimaginable torment on the party cadres assigned to the confidential goat file.

Within the party, it was the acquaintance and friendship between Changa and my father that caused the most surprise and worry. It was a thorn in the party's side. What could possibly bring these two nonparty members together, newcomers to the city, one a university-educated intellectual, the other an illiterate goatherd?

But nobody realized that it was the goats that had brought my father and Changa together. This friendship was a sore point to everyone in power—the party and the police. The party cadres responsible were afraid even to consider this friendship, because what was happening between my father and Changa was precisely what they were fighting against: a bond forged by the goats between the defeated class and the victorious one.

In the near future, the goatherds must become the working class! That is what the supreme leaders had imagined, it is what they had ordered. First, the party must prepare the people for the peaceful destruction of the goats and block any plans to the contrary. But who could stop Changa's love for the goats, for people, and for life?

Everyone feared Changa's power and influence. While they did in fact want to stop him and his goats due to the "highest interests of the party," secretly, they wanted in equal measure for Changa and his goats to stay, because they were extremely useful to the party and to the ruling powers as well. As they tried to understand, they asked themselves, What connected my father and Changa? What sort of conspiracy were they hatching? The party functionaries specializing in the goat question well knew what the illiterate Changa could do with the goats, but they had not considered what he could do if he became literate, armed with new knowledge about the goats. They wrote strictly confidential reports based on the information they often received through secret channels about the anticlass alliance between my father and Changa, the intellectual and the goatherd.

The young party members, hungry for rapid advancement in their careers, went furthest in their speculations. They knew even the titles of Father's books in Changa's possession. Had they wished, they could have rid themselves once and for all of my father and his friendship with Changa solely on the basis of a list of his books.

He could easily have been charged with possessing pro-Western propaganda and spreading capitalist ideas. Others, incidentally, had been held accountable for possession of a single Western book. Yes, they could easily have settled things with my father, but they were afraid of Changa.

My father was, of course, not so naive as to be ignorant of where danger lay; instinctively, he could always somehow sense it, even when he had no concrete evidence. He valued Changa's sincerity, his sense of reality, his oneness with life, and his intuition to detect evil, the tracks of the devil.

For days on end, Changa read Father's books about goats and their connection with life, while there before his eyes, those white goddesses gathered the green covering of the earth. Accustomed to Changa's presence, the goats calmly grazed.

Lost in his reading, he would forget about the real-life goats. Some would wander off, other goatherds would bring them back, and Changa, as a sign of thanks, would read new things aloud from the books. He once told my father that he regretted not having learned to read as a child; he had lost a whole lifetime. My father said that he, not Changa, was the one who had lost an entire lifetime—of real life—by reading his books. Perhaps it was this acknowledgment of different, though complementary, gaps in their lives that brought them together.

Over time, Changa became increasingly excited by Father's intention to write *The History of the Balkans through the Collapse of Its Empires*, in which the goats would also play a role, and he hoped he would have some part in Father's book.

One evening, Changa listened with delight as my father, enraptured, told him how goats had successfully passed through the Roman, Byzantine, and Ottoman Empires and now had managed to break a path even through Stalin's empire as well. My father was concerned lest Changa be led astray by reading and turn into a Balkan Don Quixote who, on account of ideas from his books, became too removed from life itself. (For himself, he figured, there was no hope.)

That evening, my father began thoughtfully: "Throughout the course of the history of the Balkans, the goat has appeared and disappeared among people, nations, and empires . . ."

"When did it appear, and when did it disappear?" Changa interrupted him immediately.

My father carefully examined the row of books from his library about the Balkan empires, then continued in a lofty tone, as if forgetting Changa's question: "We humans, my dear friend Changa, have since time immemorial shared a common dream with goats and other domesticated animals. Time has passed, and progress has taken us further and further from our ancestors, but our common dream endures. People are never freed from that dream, and when least expected, it returns to remind people of their close relationship."

"But the goats, what happened with the goats?" asked Changa anxiously.

"It is the goats that remind us most of our shared ancestral dream with animals," my father continued spiritedly. "Man has struggled in vain, consciously or unconsciously, to forget, destroy within him, the animal part of that dream. Those were difficult times for man on this planet. Man does not separate easily from his original nature. The goats, more vividly than any other species, have returned him to the truth of that common dream."

"Things have gotten so mixed up over time!" Changa cried.

"Yes, everything is mixed up, really mixed up!"

"But now the goats are bringing man back to his original dream, to their ancient unity; they are saving him."

My father agreed with this as well.

Changa understood more and more clearly how my father interpreted the return of people to goats in these cursed times, a time when the seed of discord had been sown, when the goats were saving adults and children alike, when the goats awakened in people their shared dream of long ago.

When Changa wanted to say something important about the goats, he would always look with fascination at the etching of the goat suckling the lion cub.

My father, without intending to, interrupted him and showed him another drawing in which, beside a mother exhausted from her household chores, a goat was rocking a baby in its cradle. Changa could only repeat, "Is it really possible? Can it really be true?"

Father continued talking on the same theme: "Whenever the beastly dream awoke here in our cursed Balkans, whenever empires changed and fratricidal wars spread, the goats—those goddesses among people—were the only ones to return people to their common dream . . ."

Changa stood and went toward the books about the Balkan empires; he began to leaf through them, looking at the illustrations. He marveled at the varied scripts. Now he regretted that he was literate in only one language and had not learned the languages of the other Balkan peoples.

My father sensed the question Changa wished to ask. "Deep down, at the very depth of our memory, there exist lost and forgotten celebrations that hold the moment of our creation, the forging of our common destiny. Perhaps the goats remind us of those celebrations . . ."

Changa did not continue Father's line of thinking; he spoke following the course of his own thoughts: "A lion never attacks a lion, or a tiger, a tiger . . . Only man kills man."

"When a person is wounded, he is carried off on a stretcher; when a lion is wounded, however, it attacks with all its strength," added my father.

"Why is that?" asked Changa.

"When he is in mortal danger, man thinks of God. Animals have no God, no remembrance of the past; they have only the present. They live in a single moment."

"Death can cause great anxiety for people. But animals don't feel that," Changa said in wonder.

"Children don't either, until they are aware that death exists. Until then, they live in their paradise. When their childhood ends, so too does their paradise!"

"So, because our children and goats don't feel that death exists, it helps create the boundless love between them," concluded Changa.

My father and Changa gathered new proofs to expand their thesis that goats appeared in the history of the Balkan nations when man invoked them in the name of some former common dream. This occurred when hate flared between people, when they were weighed down with division, strife, and the darkness of their history.

The ungrateful souls of all those well-fed people who were ready to be free of the goat, as if freed of some ugly, base, and greedy animal, revolted Changa.

"Isn't that in the very nature of human beings?" mused Changa. My father and Changa also gathered evidence about the goat's worth, its usefulness throughout history and in the present, especially the present, because they were aware of the great plot being hatched against the goats.

They searched for local and universal evidence. For local evidence, here was the indestructible goatherd Changa, hardened in his many battles to rescue the goats during the war and afterward.

My father concerned himself with universal, worldwide evidence of the goats' great worth. Together, he and Changa, consciously or unconsciously, were erecting high fortress walls around the goats to save them from the impending blows of the party and the government.

They were both well acquainted with the Balkan mentality, with its ingrained syndrome of self-destruction, a curse driving an individual or a people with goats, for whom things were going well, to wish—for no real particular reason—the death of their neighbor's goat. And so, for Changa, each book from Father's library, plus the books about goats he found through his own sources, represented a precious stone in their great fortress. There was no end to Changa's joy when he discovered in one of the books that in India the goat is a symbol both of the primordial substance—*prakriti*—and mother of the world. He wondered why the goat was connected with thunder in China. Ties between goats and divinities fascinated him, and he was delighted by some myths describing how goats playing near smoke discovered the oracle of Delphi

Changa was pleased when he discovered among Father's books a text by the ancient Latin poet from Verona, Catullus, with illustrations of the Roman forum, in which goats were roaming freely. He thought these illustrations particularly significant, because one day, he would show them to the leaders of our city.

At the end of each of their meetings, Changa would typically beg my father to give him a book from his library to read to the goatherds. My father was happy that the messages within his books, gathered through the course of his whole lifetime, were now reaching new readers—listeners from among the goatherds. That evening, he gave Changa the collection by Alphonse Daudet containing his famous story "Mr. Seguin's Goat."

9

After finishing Alphonse Daudet's story about Mr. Seguin's goat, Changa could not sleep. He was shaken to the core by the fate of the goat that speaks up and asks her owner to let her go into the mountains, to freedom. The poor thing does not know what dangers lurk in the mountains, what kind of wolfish domain rules there.

Seguin did not want to lose his goat, so he shut her in a dark stall with a double lock, but he forgot the opened window. The little goat would quickly find her way to the mountains.

The leaves of the chestnuts caress her bright white wool as she moves like a queen through the leafy green shadows. In the distance, the eyes of the sun sparkle green through the alders.

The little goat reaches her mountain heaven. The whole mountain rejoices with her. Perhaps just once in a lifetime is one touched by such great happiness.

The little goat feasts on the succulent leaves and grass.

"O how happy the little goat is," Changa said aloud, riveted by the unfolding events. "But something will happen," said Changa sadly, and he considered stopping his reading, but the fate of the goat propelled him. His fellow goatherds felt the same later when Changa read them the story. Some of them supported Seguin's actions; others did not. Changa, wise man that he was, did not take sides. He let the story's ending speak for itself; he was in no rush. Had the little goat been in the Balkan Mountains, her fate would have been different. When Changa first read it, he had not imagined that a wolf would be tangled up in this story. But the wolf quickly appeared. Changa was most impressed by the little goat's bravery and her love of freedom. Our Balkan goats— like many of their owners—have never fully freed themselves from fear. This worried Changa a great deal. Yes, Seguin's humble little goat did not know fear.

The goatherds later explained this to Changa: fear transferred from the people to their Balkan goats. He thought about the goats wandering the Roman forum, and later he pushed for the goats to roam freely in our city as well. This drove the party cadres responsible for the goats to distraction; but the goats did what goats do. The municipal party functionaries consoled themselves with the thought that the day would come when the goats and the goatherds would pay for this; an end would come at last to this cursed season of goats. They also threatened Changa, who, in their view, was reading bourgeois Western literature to the goatherds. They had their sympathizers hidden among the goatherds to whom Changa read. Later, in committee meetings, they attempted to piece together a mosaic of truth based on confused evidence, but in their powerlessness, all they could do was shout, "Who is this Mr. Segen with the goat? This is pure bourgeois propaganda. Western literature about the poisoning of goatherds, future members of the working class . . ."

But the story did not end here; there was both denouement and epilogue.

The wolf had entered the plot. Who could allow such a fate? Changa thought of the Balkans, of Stalin.

The little goat went along her way; from a distance she saw Mr. Seguin's house, her recent prison. She was at the peak of her happiness.

Changa worried about her fate, even though the wolf had not yet appeared before her eyes. "She lost her balance from so much joy and happiness," Changa added while reading.

The goat leaped high on the ridge, drawn by the instinct of her wild ancestors; far away in the distance she could see Mr. Seguin's house growing smaller, smaller, now a mere dot.

While he was reading this part of the story to the goatherds, Changa was so drawn into the events and embellished them to such a degree that at some point the goatherds could not tell what was Daudet's story and what were Changa's additions.

The day's reign was coming to its end. The first stars announced the kingdom of night. In the wink of an eye the mountain lost its daytime smile; it turned from deep blue to black. In the distance one could hear the gentle ringing of the goats returning to their folds.

With the dying rays of the day, the little goat lost her joyfulness. Far in the distance she could just make out the wisp of smoke rising from the chimney in Mr. Seguin's house. Inside, he was mourning; his soul held a gaping wound for this last goat that has abandoned him.

Night falls; quiet envelops the remains of the day. Once more, Seguin's voice echoes.

Silence. Surely his goat would change her mind, and he would hear her penitent, pitiful bleating.

The goatherds were frightened as they listened to Changa's vivid reading. Their thoughts flew to their goats. They gathered the smaller ones around them; the others were there with them as well.

Changa wanted to calm the goatherds, and he told them that this was just a simple story having nothing to do with their goats.

But they were not so naive as to believe this, because Changa's voice was also quavering.

The reading of this cursed story awakened in Changa the ominous presentiment that, after the time of the goats, there could come the time of the wolves.

He tried in vain to free himself from these ominous thoughts, but he, too, was powerless to change the fate of Seguin's little goat.

The wolf was there, and nothing could be done. Her fate was sealed.

Changa had to reveal to the goatherds the wolf's entry into the story. The goatherds looked at him sadly, wondering whether he could get past the wolf. But Changa could not change the course of events.

The little goat could have bleated loudly for Seguin to give her shelter. But the tether, fence, and prison would again await her. Seguin's final shout to his little goat faded in the silence. The little goat said farewell to any hope of return. Her only hope now was to wait for the coming day, the rising of the sun. The heartbroken goatherds hoped for this as well.

The nearby leaves rustle. Something pierces the night silence. The little goat senses the presence of the wolf. The denseness of the wild forest spreads out before her.

The wolf calmly observes his certain victim. Now, for the first time, the little goat feels lost forever.

She remembers her sister goats; she thinks of old Renaude, who fought the evil wolf the whole night long only to be devoured by him in the morning. She thinks for a moment about giving herself up to the wolf right away so as not to prolong her agony.

The goatherds were sad, and this course of events brought tears to the eyes of the soft-hearted among them. Some of them were so filled with doubt that they asked Changa to show them exactly where the author had written that the wolf was preparing to attack the little goat, even though they themselves could not read it. Here, said Changa, pointing his finger at the words.

The beast draws near; the little goat proudly stands on guard, her horns poised.

She will fight in the name of all goats, in the name of these humble goatherds listening to Changa at their head—better to struggle than to lose her freedom. Freedom has its price, even death.

"Seguin's little goat had a brave heart. Believe me, the wolf had to pause ten times in his attack to catch his breath and gather his strength," read Changa, and he proudly showed them where this was written in the book. The goatherds' self-assurance returned, and one sensed that these goats and goatherds would one day find themselves facing the wolves of our era without contemplating defeat.

While the wolf gathered new strength, the little goat savored a few more succulent blades of deep-rooted grass, as if she were drinking strength from the depths of the earth.

"The earth, the very roots were on the little goat's side," added Changa.

The frightened goatherds were silent; they begged and implored Changa to stop there and not read to the end of the story. But Changa continued. He encouraged Blanchette to hold out against the wolf's new attacks. As they gazed at the nightly dance of the stars, the goatherds, fortified by the earth's juices from those last blades of grass that the little goat had nibbled, looked toward the sky as if begging some divinity to keep the brave little goat alive until the new day dawned.

"The stars extinguished one by one," Changa read sadly. The goatherds listened with tears in their eyes. Some of the goatherds saw tears in the eyes of their goats, or at least it appeared that way.

The little goat bucked her horns one last time, but the wolf sharpened his bloodthirsty fangs.

A pale light appeared on the horizon. The sun struggled to break through.

"The sun is coming up, the sun is coming up," repeated the goatherds.

In the distance, the crowing of a rooster was heard. The sun was indeed rising. But it was too late!

As the day dawned in the distance, the little goat no longer waited to be saved but to unite with the sun and with eternity. She lay down on the ground in her white coat, stained with blood.

The goatherds stood up as if they, too, wanted to be part of the story's epilogue. They hugged their goats. For the first time in their lives, they saw Changa brush away tears. They looked at the sky, now clouded over. A great lightning bolt flashed and for a brief second lit the sky.

The goatherds were frightened by this flash of premature dawn. They were frightened by this apparent omen marking the end of the time of the goats appearing in the preternatural brightness of the sky. The flash of lightning announced rain. Changa put the book in his bag.

The goatherds did not want to see it again. They were not sorry that they were illiterate; some were sorry that Changa had learned to read.

10

*D*eath came and went at will in our family during times of war, resettlement, drought, and hunger; many of Mother's delicate offspring died. A newborn's fingers that had still not been held soon pulled away from Mother's withered breasts.

We all had a little brother or sister whom death had carried off, and we never got over our loss. We believed that our goat would now keep death from approaching our family whenever it wanted.

Hunger spread through the country, but in the Goatherd Quarter, a happy time was dawning with the goats. No one knew how long this time would last, but no matter how long it lasted, it was important to take advantage of it to give strength to our lives and move us from childhood to youth, from youth to adulthood.

The city awoke to yet more posters and slogans, both old and new: "Long live Socialism!" "Our future is Communism!" "Tito and Stalin are our Future!" "Death to the class enemy!" "Brotherhood and Unity!" "Death to the Speculators!" "Long live the Collectives!" "Death to . . ."

Death to this, death to that. We did not understand the meaning of these slogans. We noticed only that the more there were, the more stores were emptied, private businesses were closed, and prices rose. So we children were frightened by these new slogans. We were frightened most of all when the day dawned with a new slogan: "Death to the goats!"

My mother was nearing the end of her pregnancy, but she could not free herself of household worries and maintaining her usual order. Nearly at the limit of her capacity to give birth, she entered into an uncertain battle between the strength of her body and the life of this newborn.

After so many deaths, this birth was a strike back at fate, a way out, a renewal of hope. God seemed to keep these Balkan mothers alive longer than their infants. Dressed in black, they were the last to extinguish, like long tapers symbolizing family and life itself. When they lost a more grown-up son or daughter, they would curse God that he had not taken them. But God infused their darkened souls with new strength to endure. No one could understand the meaning of this black circle of life.

Every new birth was a holiday for the Goatherd Quarter. Every family rejoiced as much as if it were their own newborn. Life continued, new life after so many deaths in the Great War. But the waves of the war had cast up Noah's arks filled with the many families rescued from all parts of the Balkans and beyond. There were even some Sephardic Jewish families; there was an Armenian family of musicians, and a Russian family, rescued from the October Revolution; there were several Turkish families as well as several families from Aegean Macedonia; and here was our Albanian family amidst the large Macedonian population, which had landed in this small Goatherd Quarter. But also other, unknown families came and left the Goatherd Quarter. Here were intermingled nationalities, faiths, and customs; people lived in trust, understanding; together they more easily countered the blows of fate in those uncertain times.

Because the great wars and the strategies of those who waged them had not fatefully alienated them from each other, because no fratricidal war had been inflicted upon them as in other parts of the Balkans, and because they had not been conquered, there was no reason, during the time of the goats, for people not to become closer to one another, to respect one another, to suffer each death together, and to rejoice in each new life, to mingle together and celebrate each marriage and each religious holiday. There was reason for everyone to believe in this time of the goats, the most beautiful time on earth.

Mother's last newborn arrived into the world with the assistance of our closest neighbor, the old Russian woman who lived with her two sons. She was very experienced, and she loved our family as her own.

We loved her like a grandmother, because our real grandmothers had remained beyond the border, one still living, the other, deceased.

In our days of hunger, before Father had bought a goat, Baba Rusinka often called us over; she never failed to give us a piece of bread spread with cheese to nibble on and a glass of milk from her goats. Even now, during Mother's last confinement, there was our Baba Rusinka beside my mother in her battle between life and death.

As newcomers, we had no close relatives in the city. We heard Mother's muffled cries in response to her great pains. We younger children stood riveted behind the door. We were afraid someone would take our mother away. We waited for the cry of our new little brother or sister to turn Mother's pains into calming cries of joy, to turn our fear into joy. Beside us was our little kid, our good fortune, at the threshold of this newborn's life.

Our hearts were beating quickly. In these moments of birth, we were frightened by death. Death and life too often collided and, more rarely, crossed paths in the life of our family. But here were our mother and Baba Rusinka, a worthy, plump old woman, with her long, pale blond hair, her golden locks falling on her broad forehead, her thick eyebrows and kind blue eyes, guarding my mother from death.

During the war, when we were alone and my mother was younger, she would deliver the baby herself, with no one's help. But she was older now.

At last—we heard the cry we had waited for, and right away we could breathe more easily. We hugged each other, we hugged the goat, and it bleated happily. The cries of the newborn and the bleating of the goat sounded together. Baba Rusinka called us to come into the room and timidly we opened the door and went in with the goat. Mother gazed at us tenderly and fell asleep. Baba Rusinka lifted the baby, holding it with one hand by its two feet, and she said tenderly, "A baby brother, you have a baby brother, my children!"

If there is a heaven, it was here, and we were in it in those moments when we saw our mother alive together with her newborn.

For many decades, I could not find an image that captured for eternity the moment of childhood's lost paradise. Many, many years later, at an exhibit of Chagall's paintings in Paris, there on a large canvas I recognized the heavenly moment in my childhood, in the life of our uprooted family.

In the great, boundless blue of Chagall's paintings, in the blueness in which the earth and sky merge, I saw a family with goats, floating between the earth and the sky. It was not possible to determine where they were; they seemed to belong equally to the heavens and to the earth.

Yes, we children—with our happy mother and our little brother, and our goat—did not know whether we were flying toward the sky or whether the ground held us. Just as in Chagall's large canvas.

11

A new life settled into our family. It was like a holiday—a newborn holiday. This birth alone was cause for celebration after so many deaths in the family.

Whenever we lost a baby brother or sister, we expected a new birth, something in return for the brother or sister we had lost.

But later, when we had grown up a bit, we came to understand that it was not the same. A vision of our happiness was interwoven in this new beginning.

That is how we grew; every death aged us by ten years, a hundred years. My mother needed to rescue us and restore to us our family's lost time, to find some resolution; she was a victim sacrificed at the border of life and death. She was our eternal flame.

Whenever she sensed death circling about her children, my mother, poor thing, with no strength left, surrendered herself to death and fell into a deadly fever lasting for days. She had no strength left to mourn or to weep when death coldly snatched away one of her children. Her soul remained drier than a desert. The death of a child pulled her from her fevered nightmare. She would again move in our family circle, drawing out our shared chronicle of life and death. Had there been some penicillin or other antibiotic in those hopeless moments when no other cure could be found, our family's fate would have been different. As it was, everything had to be resolved in the boundless soul and tortured body of my mother, the holy protector at the gates of our uprooted family, whose fatherland was the ill-fated Balkans.

Unlike previous births, Mother's last childbirth took place when we already had a goat. It had quickly become a part of the family. We called it a *kid*, even though it was already a mature doe and had given us its first milk. Our little brother was nursed by the goat rather than by my mother, whose milk had run dry. It was a great relief and the reason this last newborn lived.

We called our little brother Agim, which means "dawn." Given our fate, my father did not want his children's names to be connected with saints, military figures, or other famous people. He said that everyone had his own destiny, and he was of a mind that his children be given names meaning *lion, light, will, wish, dawn, life . . .*

In fact, my mother was more concerned with the internal fate of the family, my father, with its external fate, but there was always firm mutual agreement between them.

As my older brothers grew up, they took on family obligations; after having completed a high school program, most often in medical or technical professions, they were employed immediately, creating opportunities for the younger ones to study at university. Most chose to study medicine.

My brothers and my sister could never forget Mother's battles to keep her children who disappeared for lack of medicines. The children who remained alive promised to study medicine to help our mother and the family.

My father thought it good for immigrant families to produce doctors who could be of help to all people and allow the family to survive more securely in these uncertain and cursed Balkan times.

It was easy for my father to influence our course of study so that we would become doctors, veterinarians, and medical staff; it was not as easy for him to protect us from the assaults of ideology, the party, and the government.

My mother blessed Socialism for opening unprecedented opportunities for her to send her children to good schools, but my father stepped anxiously along its borders. He had vast experience from past currents that had blown across the Balkans, and he had skillfully managed to protect his family from several ideologies, from Fascism to Stalinism, and from becoming entangled in religion or politics.

My father believed that following a path into politics to drag ourselves out of poverty would be a mistake, a fatal step. As a new arrival, Father had, in fact, been caught up in politics and an immigrant organization until he acquired his citizenship, and he felt lucky when he could free himself from them in order to devote himself fully to his old forgotten Ottoman manuscripts, to interpret their secrets, and to search for the keys to their meaning. At heart, he wanted his sons to be involved in politics only so far as to keep politics from being involved with them. But here, no boundaries could be established, no border set. So he abandoned this idea as well.

When one of my older brothers told him that he was a candidate for admission into the party, my father did not react negatively, as might have been expected.

My mother was nervous when she heard this, fearing it would destroy the peace they had experienced till then, the equilibrium in the family that my father, a nonparty member, had successfully maintained. She was frightened. But my father was not completely sure where he himself stood toward Communism. For him, it was an exalted ideal, but one difficult to achieve in this life, an idea easily embraced by the poor and the ignorant.

When people have no concrete solutions for their specific circumstances, they seek a way out in grand ideas. On account of these grand ideas, practical solutions are put off. This was, incidentally, also how he considered belief in God, except that this idea has been the longest lasting in the history of humankind. My father reasoned that it was impossible to have faith in two different gods. He was absolutely convinced of this.

He wanted to suggest this to his son, who was leaning toward politics, but he could not convince him. Nor did my father want to dissuade his son, any of his sons, to turn from the path they had embarked on. He did not meddle out of fear that it would have the opposite effect from the one he intended, and also because the decision was theirs. And so he was not adamant, even when it was entirely clear that he should say yes or no.

Before he was admitted to the party, my brother had to participate in a Communist youth volunteer work brigade, first in rebuilding a destroyed rail line in one of the neighboring republics, then in the construction of the Brotherhood and Unity Highway, which was to connect this country with both Europe and Asia, and finally in assisting in the construction of an artificial lake in his native republic by draining swamps.

In her heart, my mother was opposed to letting him set out along what for her were uncertain pathways. She told herself that Father's wandering Odyssean spirit had been passed on to her son. But when my father had traveled, those were uncertain times of war. She could understand why he had had to move around, because it kept him alive, but the travels her oldest son proposed were difficult for her to grasp. My father, ever faithful to his principles, did not want to prevent my brother from entering the party, yet secretly, he feared that his son would become so entranced by the party's promises that some of the other brothers would follow his example. But whatever would happen, would happen.

When the time had come for us to find a suitable name for our little goat, my father clearly saw that my brother had become deeply involved in politics. In the spirit of our family tradition to give neutral names to the children, there was no reason that an exception would be made for a goat. My brother, a future party member, knowing that we had to name our goat, cited several important figures from recent history, but since nearly all of them were men, their names could not be considered. My father, as was his custom, did not protest when my brother surprised us all with this suggestion: "Let's call it by the name of our liberator, our generalissimo—let's call it Stalinka!"

There was complete silence. The quiet was broken by the cries of our little brother, whom Mother had swaddled and set down to be nursed by the goat. He soon grew quiet. Now the rest of us children were ready to burst into tears because of the name my brother had suggested.

We all turned to our father. This was the moment for him to decide. I think even he, hand on heart, was caught by surprise. He could not immediately get over his realization that his son had become committed to a political career, in contrast to the usual slow rhythm so important for the family's survival. He searched to find in himself, in his isolation from the party and from politics, the reasons for his son's turn toward the party. Father had been completely preoccupied with the family's resettlement and the resulting consequences, and he had within him an unspoken fear lest the family not be able to take root in this new soil, because it was not easy to uproot a family bound for generations to one country and then have it adapt to the life of another.

Always afraid to make categorical decisions, his soul softened by the family's migrations and the hard knocks of fate, he now saw that his children were freed of his frustrations, but he feared that this could have the opposite effect in this new environment and destroy the moral fortress he had built.

My father was not as much concerned about his son's future development as a party member as he was by the fact that he could not understand his own response; he sought reasons for his continued neutrality, for the immigrant's readiness to compromise where, objectively, there may have been no reason to do so. We expected our father to forbid the naming of our goat Stalinka, as my brother, the party candidate, had proposed, but at that moment he could not say anything that could be interpreted as a firm opinion.

So we named our goat Stalinka. In point of fact, we children were not absolutely sure who Stalin was. Indeed, neither was my brother, the party candidate, who had suggested it.

In the large living room that served as our bedroom, we looked at Stalin's photograph hanging next to Tito's on the wall above our beds. We looked at Stalin, with his stern look, bushy eyebrows, and moustache. We believed that such power would protect our goat, our family.

12

*W*hen the party learned we had named our goat Stalinka, the hard-core ideologues among them were opposed, but they could say nothing publicly or privately because they did not want to be understood as being opposed to our "big brother." Furthermore, the party still did not want to play an active role in the goat question, and no directives for action had come down from the central party leadership, even though the goat dossier inside the iron strongbox in the municipal party secretary's office grew fatter by the day. It was likely that our little Stalinka was already in that dossier. Who could know? Father's friend Changa was a bit taken aback when he first learned our goat's name, but he never questioned Father's integrity, no matter what he heard about him. He, in turn, never understood how one of his main bucks came to be called Stalin. He had never given his permission.

In the homes of the Goatherd Quarter where there were many children, it was possible to have three, four, or even five does but almost never a buck. The leading goatherds, especially Changa, could allow themselves to keep two or three bucks, enough not only for their whole herd but for the other does as well. It was obvious, in those years of hunger, that it made no sense for anyone to maintain bucks separately for the sole satisfaction of a few goats. Even Changa could get by with two billies to take care of all the nannies in his herd, but he, like others, helped out the poor families of other goatherds.

When our Stalinka grew and became a mature doe, she sometimes acted strangely, and a certain restlessness took hold of her. She gave less milk and would suddenly dart from the house when she could sense other goats—especially a billy—being led to the wild part of the park. We stopped her from running away, but we did not know what was happening. We felt sad for our Stalinka; we did not know what was bothering her. But once, when Changa was going past our house with his herd, our Stalinka sensed the does and bucks from a distance, and she bolted toward them. Then it was clear to all of us. It was time for us to take Stalinka to the bucks. That's what the children from the neighboring houses did with their goats. Ours was no exception, and we settled down once we had figured out the cause of our dear Stalinka's restlessness.

It was a Sunday afternoon in spring. A free day. We had spent nearly the whole week before getting ready to accompany our goat to Changa's herd. He was Father's friend, and we believed he would help get the job done quickly.

We woke early that day, with the first crowing of the roosters. We went outside. Stalinka was awake, ready to go, impatient. We brushed her nicely. We scented her with perfume from a little bottle my mother never used. We placed a garland of flowers from Mother's garden around her neck.

We set off to the bucks.

Changa was up and about. The nannies had been let out of their stalls into the spacious yard at Changa's house. He noticed us from a distance and hurried to open the door.

The goats nibbled the remains of hay left out for them earlier. The few billies were kept a bit of a distance from the nannies. Two younger ones with shaggy white and golden hair playfully tested their strength by butting together their long, curly horns. One of the older bucks noticed our Stalinka. Her old restlessness was back, even stronger than before. Changa warmly greeted us and gave us some warm goat milk. He guessed our problem immediately. We were embarrassed and did not know how to tell him why we had come. He laughed and, to put us at ease, asked after our father and our family. In the Goatherd Quarter, there were other bucks and does with names connected with Stalin, but we had not known that Changa's lead buck, the one who had first caught sight of our Stalinka, was among them.

Our goat caught Stalin's eye, and she began to twirl her tail; she tugged at the tether we had tied around her neck.

To distract our attention, Changa spoke to us about other things. With a strong tug, Stalinka freed herself from the tether.

Changa gave us a sign to let her go. That big, robust buck frightened us. Our little goat may have been tender and powerless when we named her Stalinka, but Changa's lusty buck certainly deserved the name Stalin.

The buck was a true giant, with a strong, protruding neck, big horns ready to fly off like arrows, and a rugged jaw. Stalinka moved shyly, then playfully, toward the buck. He leaped where he stood, turned around once, twice, then rose on his hind legs, twisting his robust body. Changa's goats kept off to the side, frightened; they did not want to feel Stalin's unrestrained body upon theirs so early in the morning—they were well acquainted with Stalin's grip. Some goats had hardly survived, barely held on to their lives after their long, intoxicating embrace with that unbridled buck.

Changa's goats seemed to know the routine and did not react when Stalin suddenly dashed off and stopped in front of this unfamiliar goat. Stalinka took her first, tentative steps, but when we saw the buck, we wanted to go and get her back. It was too late. The buck stood poised on his hind hooves, like a white love god. Stalinka gently moved toward him, aroused as if she were an experienced lover, not a virgin. With her tender lips and flaring nostrils, her long tongue like a red flame, she lit up the air as she touched the buck. The buck, afire, turned in the air and, leaping up like an acrobat, grasped Stalinka in his wide embrace. His two forehooves enveloped her whole head, and with his hind legs he pulled Stalinka's rosy behind to him. They stayed joined a few moments.

Looking at Stalinka under the body of the great buck, we children were ready to burst into tears, run over to free her, save our Stalinka from the buck's grasp. But Changa held us back. When the buck moved off, we rushed toward Stalinka. She had never been so calm, and she gently opened her eyes. We were happy our goat was now pregnant and would give birth to a goat for us, but we were happier still that she was saved, with no serious consequences, from Stalin's potent grip. We were lucky that our Stalinka had survived. We were happy that Stalin himself had impregnated her, and perhaps one day, we, too, would have a strong buck.

The sun's rays lit up the horizon. Changa's goats were ready to go out to pasture toward the river and the hills. The bucks went first, with Stalin in the lead. The does walked tranquilly behind them.

And we set off behind Changa's herd with our happy Stalinka. Changa was also happy. It showed in his generous and tender look, his human ray that warmed our souls.

13

*W*e marched along proudly with Changa's goats and with our Stalinka, as if we had scored some victory, though over whom we did not know. Until yesterday, we had watched sadly and longingly from our house as this column of goats, led by Changa and his bucks, had passed by; now we were a part of it . . .

It seemed as if Changa had within him an unerring compass with which he sensed the direction of natural history. He was nature personified, and his love for the goats was a part of his nature.

Changa well knew that these white animals—with their tender glances and heavy bodies giving proof of their fecundity—were always ready to suck the juices from the black earth and turn it into white milk. When he saw his fellow mountain dwellers forced to come down into the city with their goats in order to take up heavy tools and become an iron-forged working class, Changa felt that someone was intentionally trying to turn the world's natural order upside down. Deep down, he simply could not agree with this new regime: Why did it disperse the houses, properties, and families and then recombine them in new, un-natural ways—in collectives—and then force the remaining mountain dwellers, who had nothing to part with except their goats, to come down into the cities and become a new working class overnight?

Changa felt that it was a great misfortune that these new conquerors intended to sketch out a plan for Socialism, then throw it at the people as if for their past mistakes.

Changa was a man tied to the rhythm and breathing of the mountains, the brooks, and the thunder, but even here in this cursed city, he maintained his instinct for life's pulse. He was as steadfast as a river. He had brought the goats to the city together with the people, and he did not want to abandon them halfway.

We watched Changa here, in this part of the valley, in the wondrous pastoral landscape, thoughtful beside his playful goats. We were here for the first time with his goats and with our Stalinka. As soon as the other goatherds would catch sight of Changa from a distance, they would come with their herds to pass the time with him. If they sensed that he was in the right mood, they would begin a conversation with him about the goats or ask him to read something about goats from Father's books.

At that time, Changa was reading books about goats from all over the world to discover the true place of the domestic Balkan goat. He told the goatherds about the Kashmir goat from Mongolia and Tibet whose wool was spun into rich cashmere yarn. The goatherds were amazed by a goat found in the Caucasus that always gives birth to two kids at a time. They asked Changa why, but he could not give them a full explanation, and he drew their attention to the Angora goat, famous in Turkey, Iran, Pakistan, Russia, Australia, and America. The goatherds listened in wonder; some of them were hearing about these countries for the first time, and until then, none of them had ever heard of the Maltese, Apennine, and Mediterranean goats. The goatherds then asked Changa to tell them about Seguin's goat; they remained forever upset by her tragic fate. They could not get over the loss of Seguin's little goat, which had been eaten by the wolf; they feared other wolves themselves.

Today, Changa had no time for the goatherds. He went off into the white silence of the mountain. Clearly, some new thought was burning inside him. As his thoughts formed, his broad forehead would crease in new wrinkles and then relax. The goatherds knew how to interpret the quiet that radiated from Changa. They left him there in his tranquility, like the sky before a lightning storm. In these uncertain times, when everything could change and darken as quickly as clouds could descend on a mountain, when the seed of discord could easily be sown and take root in the soul of the people, when a directive could come from "the other sky" to change everything and turn everything to black, Changa's white ray of calm remained the people's last hope.

In the distance, the red eye of the sun was setting, and the clouds scattered to all sides like a lost herd. When the evening star began to twinkle, Changa headed for the city with his contented, sated goats. He looked once more toward the sky, but he could not clear his thoughts as he had in the morning pasture. The nannies walked toward the city, with the billies now behind them. The goats knew the route by themselves. Sometimes Changa would let them go, and they would make their own way home.

We had spent a wonderful day with Changa, the goats, and the goatherds. The other children from the Goatherd Quarter looked at us enviously as we strode past them with Changa's herd. As we were passing, we stopped in front of our house by the river, and in our great joy, we began to sing, so everyone would hear us singing the song we heard most often at that time but whose meaning we did not know or understand either then or later:

America and England will be proletarian lands!

Changa smiled, and we marched along with a refrain we didn't fully understand on our lips and then entered into our long courtyard with Stalinka at our heels. Our parents had come out and were standing in the doorway, visibly worried about our full-day absence. Changa greeted them, and my father invited him in for a drink. Changa accepted, and the goats continued by themselves on the path toward home.

My father climbed the wooden steps to the balcony with Changa behind him, while out in the yard, our song continued. My mother brought *rakija* to drink and some *meze*, wiped off the table, and went out.

"The poor proletariats could have reached America and England with their goats, but where will we end up?" Changa began.

"Joking aside, with Stalin one doesn't know. Things are not going well," Father said, immediately changing the course of the conversation.

"With Stalin or without him, we are staying with our goats!" Changa interrupted.

"But independent of Stalin," my father continued. "Here in our country, 'plans for a new Socialist order' will not be delayed, and they will engulf our goats as well."

"I sense bad times coming, too. After all, how long can luck last in the Balkans? They will find someone to give the order to kill off our goats. And who else but one of us," Changa said thoughtfully.

"That's how it is, Changa! We are our own worst enemies."

"But we won't just sit here with arms folded!"

"If they say to destroy the goats, it will be difficult for someone to stop them."

"We will see, we will see . . ." Changa concluded.

A long silence set in.

They exchanged thoughts without saying a word. It was time for a certain foreign radio broadcast intended for listeners in our country. My father searched for the shortwave station on the peacock-shaped radio. The chime sounded, and the program began. Right at the start, the announcer mentioned Tito and Stalin. My father and Changa listened with concern. They sensed that new waves of history were going to pound our country. We children fell asleep, blessed by our happy tiredness.

My father and Changa walked about the room long into the night, searching, combing through the books.

My mother, nearly exhausted from the recent birth, had resumed her old work rhythm and again followed my father's sleepless nights. She, too, sensed that something significant was happening, or she had at least an inkling.

14

*T*he Goatherd Quarter was in a frenzy as everyone anticipated a death sentence for the goats. The streets remained empty, the children sad, the goats hidden in basements. Fear reigned, just as it does before war breaks out. The people stored provisions; there was not much to be had, but they put together as much as possible for the dark days ahead.

Without the goats, we were sure to go hungry. Once it was learned that the party was preparing special measures against the goats, there was a danger that the old, nearly forgotten quarrels would begin again.

Fear settled into all our childhoods. Although in poor families, fear enters one door and goes out the other, we were nearly defeated from thinking that someone could take away our goats and kill them. This fear would linger a long time in those who kept goats. For days, we did not bring the goats to pasture. The last drops of milk were squeezed from them. The city quickly emptied; the white whirl vanished. The great wait began.

One morning, the word "Census, census, census!" echoed through the Goatherd Quarter and the city.

The news reached our family as well.

"Now what kind of census is this, for heaven's sake; wasn't there a census in the fall?" asked my mother aloud, setting aside her knitting as she sat on the balcony beside my father, who was leafing through an old book. He slowly set the book aside and took off his glasses, but before he could respond to Mother's words, my brother the party member rushed out onto the balcony, calling from a distance, "There is going to be a census, a census of all the goats; it's an order from the supreme party leadership. The government has to get it organized quickly."

My father was considered a well-informed person. Throughout the night, he listened to local and foreign radio stations, both Western and Eastern. Sometimes, he listened until the small hours of the morning, and he would then put together his understanding of the truth. He was a calm person; he did not fall easily into traps of enthusiasm or optimism. He was too well informed ever to be an optimist. Only the ill-informed are optimists, he would often tell us. Except for our family and Changa, there was no one with whom he could share his thoughts. He somehow compensated for that by listening to the voices on the radio. He often commented aloud about significant news items as if entering into conversation with absent interlocutors.

My father, an immigrant to the city, without kith or kin (not counting the goats, those foreign creatures who had, over time, shared so much with us that they had become part of our family), thought it unwise to get mixed up in local politics—having in mind my brother the party member—because even when we were right about something, it was difficult for others to put trust in us. Yet when my older brother did get involved in politics, my father was the one who became his main advisor, tempering his enthusiasms, strong reactions, hasty judgments, and illusions.

My oldest brother's news about the census brought the whole family out onto the balcony.

Mother was the first to break the silence: "A census of the goats. That can't be a good thing."

"They want to see how many goats we have and then—the knife!" said one of my older brothers.

We younger ones, when we learned of the upcoming goat census, had tears ready to flow down our cheeks at any moment. My father did not say anything immediately, but his look, the calm radiating from his blue eyes, soothed us again, even though death was already knocking on the doors of the houses in the Goatherd Quarter.

All sorts of ideas and foreboding took hold of us. The goats were almost completely joined with our lives.

Never in these parts of the Balkans had man drawn so close, joined so completely with any animal. The instinct for self-preservation in the goats and the people merged into an indestructible collective resistance.

At other times, Father passed on to us information from the old books he had gathered from all parts of the Balkans and other countries as well about how nearly all the peoples of the Balkans owed their lives to the goats. He had once told Changa, "If the history of the Balkan goats were written, it would be one of the best histories of the Balkan nations."

In the Goatherd Quarter, rumors about the goat census spread, multiplied, and changed form. No one knew any longer what kind of census it was. But one morning, as soon as the census commission teams began entering the houses where goats were kept, everything became clear. Once the census began, a grave silence settled into the Goatherd Quarter, like that at a funeral with no end.

My mother was already on her feet at dawn. She had a routine that she had created over the years. Out in the garden, first the flower blossoms would greet her, then the shine of color on some newly ripened fruit, and finally, our three goats.

The census takers met my mother as she was watering the flowers in her garden with water from the well. She quickly led them to the balcony.

We children were long since awake; we could not sleep. My mother gave each of the census takers a small dish of mulberry fruit preserves and cold water. Then my father came in from his study. He greeted them. We children came, too, from the goats after we thought we had them well hidden and had left them enough leaves.

The census team had three members. It was not hard for us to figure out who was the leader—it was usually the one who had a leather coat and, as a rule, a moustache. People with leather coats and moustaches were usually from the police, the government, or the party. Both the law and the administration of justice were in their hands. One word from them could change the life of any family. Our frightened young eyes were turned toward the person in the long black coat and the big moustache, which gave him a stern appearance, even when a reserved smile appeared on his face. In order to pull himself away from our fixed stares and to lessen the tension, he turned to us first and said with un-natural kindness, "What are you so afraid of, children? This is just a census, an ordinary census. Only instead of people, we are counting goats. What is there here to be afraid of? The state wants to know what it has at its disposal."

These unexpected words spoken by the leader of the group eased our anxiety. Our youngest brother, wiping his tears, asked first, "Uncle, you aren't going to kill our little goats, are you?"

"Of course not, little one, we aren't killing goats."

"You aren't going to take them away from us?"

"No, no, we are just conducting a brief census," the leader answered, and he looked toward the second-in-command, who quickly took from his tattered leather case several multicolored census lists and a large yellow account book. We easily recognized them as the same sheets from the last census of our family, and that quickly calmed us.

Mother served another round of preserves to the members of the commission, and the leader took a sip of mulberry *rakija*.

My father thoughtfully looked out the large balcony window; his gaze seemed to move with the flow of the river. Such feelings always took hold of him during the resettlements of his younger years. But now it was difficult to escape from this Balkan cage; it was possible for a person only to fling himself into another cage, which was, in most cases, just like this one. He saw the impending events unfolding while we lived through these moments, temporarily reassured by his words.

The stern voice of the second member of the commission broke the silence.

"We will now inform you about the census. This is the main book," he said, indicating the large yellow account book, "and these are the census forms, one for each goat."

We had been calmed by the leader's words, but now the second member of the team filled us once again with fear.

My father calmly anticipated the words of the census taker, who warned him that the family must provide accurate information; if the questions were not answered truthfully, there would be legal consequences. These words were enough to frighten us children completely. We huddled close to our mother. The leader noticed and interrupted his subordinate.

"This family is quite familiar with the law. Move on to the questions."

This calmed us down again, but now my father's face took on a concerned look. We thought that the census taker seemed confused. The leader chided him: "Get going with the questions, because we have a lot of work ahead of us; there are many goats in the Goatherd Quarter."

"Shared misfortune is less misfortune!" my mother said quietly, mainly to herself, but in those moments, we children absorbed the very quiet, and we understood what she had in mind.

The official put on his glasses and in a raised tone asked the first question: "Family name?"

My father, instead of answering, asked, "Which family do you mean?"

The chief immediately burst in: "Careful, you blockhead, these are the lists for the census of people, not goats. How many times do I need to tell you?"

My father suppressed a smile. Only we children noticed it. We thought events were taking a lucky turn.

The official looked at the paper in confusion. He could not figure out how to alter these sheets left from the last census of people to carry out a goat census. His boss's stern look confused him even more. Finally, he pulled himself together and continued questioning my father: "How many goats do you have?"

"Three!"

"First and last name, and father's name?"

Laughter filled the room. We children were laughing too. One of us said, "Our goats have only first names!"

The leader could not restrain himself. "Of course, goats only have first names. This is what happens when the census office assigns us illiterate cadres."

He was furious and continued to ask the questions himself without even looking at the paper, because in all likelihood, he was not so literate himself. After all, it was his job to lead the group, not to read and ask questions. But he knew all the questions by heart, he had repeated them so many times, and so he continued to ask as though he were reading: "Names of the goats?"

"Brighty, Stalinka, and Ugly," my father answered.

The second official wrote down the names while pronouncing them loudly: "Briii-ghty, Staaalii," . . . but the leader immediately cut him off and turned to my father sternly: "I do not understand the reason for that order—Stalinka, then Ugly. I do not understand."

My mother immediately cut in: "Brighty, so our day will always be bright; she came to us like a gift from God. Stalinka came to us when I gave birth to my last child. So many of my children had died. When we bought the third, she was a real beauty, and we did not want our protector, Stalinka, to catch the evil eye, so we named her Ugly. With the name Ugly we wanted to protect Stalinka, and with Stalinka our children."

The leader looked in confusion at my mother. He did not know how to continue with the census, so he said, "My dear people, every-thing is confused in this family. Who has ever heard of a nanny bearing the name of the nation's great liberator? If it had at least been a buck.

No, no, what am I saying, not even a buck. You have a portrait of Stalin. Stalin is our brother, whatever happens. There are varied opinions. Stalin liberated us. His name is sacred to all of us!"

"And for us, the goats are sacred!" my mother parried.

"I understand, I understand, but still, a goat is a goat."

A new wave of quiet set in. A new wave of fear. We were all afraid Father would respond with an attack on Stalin. There had been such incidents. Ever since my brother the party member had decided that we should call our goat Stalinka, this danger had existed. Now a danger existed that the census would end ominously not only for the goats but for the family as well. The leader consulted with the third member of the commission, who was always silent, and then he continued: "Listen, folks, your goat Stalinka cannot be entered onto any census list."

Just as misery is doled out in various portions, just about equal for the majority of the population, so too is fear. The higher the place in the hierarchy of this government, the greater the fear. Among poor people, fear seemed to be conquerable. The chief surely wanted to share his dose of fear with the third member, and he continued, "The name Stalinka for a goat could be interpreted in different ways. The lists reach higher levels of leadership, all the way to the federal leaders. For one simple name, many heads could roll. Give it another name, so we can all rest easy. Give it any name you want . . . just not Stalinka."

We could not forget the day when our brother the party member had proposed it and Father had consented to name our goat Stalinka, even though he was generally true to his principle that we free ourselves from names of military leaders, saints, and liberators and pick names of flowers and other names from nature. We looked at our brother the party member, who was searching for something to say; he finally burst out energetically, "Instead of Stalinka, write down Liberty, because Stalin means liberty for us!"

The leader beamed with satisfaction and said, "Son, you will go far if you join the party!"

"I am already a member!" my brother proudly confirmed.

The leader, now completely satisfied, handed the census form once again to the second-in-command: "Write down Liberty, and be careful you don't get the questions mixed up again."

"Gender?" the official continued.

"Female, of course!" the leader interrupted again.

"Well, it could have been a billy goat!" the official said, speaking in his own defense for the first time.

"For the billies, we take our goats to Changa the goatherd, across the Wooden Bridge," said one of the younger brothers. The official once again fell into his earlier confusion. The leader looked at him sternly, waiting for him to continue.

"Nationality?"

Now my father laughed. We children sprang to life.

My brother the party member, emboldened by the chief's earlier praise, was the first to answer: "Balkan!"

"Balkaaan!" wrote down the chief.

"Goats do not have nationalities. Goats have breeds. Ask what breed it is!" proposed the leader to him in a whisper.

"Nationality is not important, but breed is. What breed are your goats?"

"They are Saanens," answered my father.

The second official pushed on again: "Religious affiliation?"

The chief again exploded: "You donkey, goats don't have religion!"

My mother whispered, "Yes they do, they have faith, sometimes more than people."

"Age of the goats?" continued the official.

"Unknown!"

"Color of the goats and any distinguishing marks?"

"Brighty is totally white; Stalinka, or Liberty, is white with a brown neck; and Ugly is white with black spots."

The census taker completed his questions.

"Somehow or other we have finished our business!" the leader said at last with satisfaction, and he took a last sip of *rakija*. On the way out, he muttered, "It would have gone quicker if we did not have so many illiterates in our ranks . . ."

15

*W*hen Father whispered in secret to my mother, "Stalin is done for," we immediately thought about our poor little Stalinka. With tears in our eyes, we went out to see her, to stroke her hair, to hug her. Stalinka, as always, greeted us serenely and tenderly and then turned her gaze back toward the succulent grasses.

For us, the quarrel between Tito and Stalin was important because it was connected to our goats, especially our Stalinka. We tried to overhear other things my father whispered about Stalin following the most recent news.

My mother's reaction was always the same: "As long as there is no war, as long as there is no war!"

We quickly stopped calling Stalinka by her name. She was accustomed to her name, however, so when we did not use it, she treated us differently. In our young minds, we feared that if we used her name too often, Stalinka would be the first to be taken away and slaughtered.

With the news concerning the end of good relations between Tito and Stalin, the time of the goats' demise was approaching. Everyone was anxious about it, the whole Goatherd Quarter, the city, the country, but because of our Stalinka, we worried more than the others. It was possible that they would take the goats away or kill them, but because of Stalinka, our family could be punished. We worked out all kinds of plans to save our goats, beginning with Stalinka. We wanted to take a large amount of food and hide in the nearby mountain caves with our goats; we could live awhile on goat milk, and then, when things calmed down, we would return to the city when freedom returned as well. We could not comprehend what terrible thing the goats had done for them to be killed now. After all, as anyone could read in Father's books, people had survived precisely because of the goats. What had happened to these people? But for us, the Goatherd Quarter had grown into our white fortress of life in the shadow of the great stone fortress. Mothers pulled their children out of death's embrace with the milk of these goats. In the Balkans, this love between people and goats was pure, complete, and holy. With the goats, people of different faiths and nationalities drew closer more easily. In the postwar years of Communism, the more these people were assured that God did not exist, the more they believed that God did exist through these goats, sent here for life to continue.

Every family in the Goatherd Quarter who kept goats concocted every possible plan to save the goats, individually and collectively. In our family, as soon as Father went to work, we children began to turn on the radio more frequently, hoping to be the first to learn any news about the destruction of the goats and to be the first to do something about it. At that time, our parents did not talk about the goats, so as not to alarm or sadden us. But one morning, it finally happened; the radio broadcast the first news about the end of the goats.

"The goats," echoed the speaker's energetic voice, "are sworn enemies of Socialism. Because of the goats, our glorious working class would never be able to reach Communism. The goats are destroying Socialist public lands: the mountains, the forests. Therefore, we must collectively destroy them . . ."

These words from the radio were like poisonous arrows piercing our souls. Even though we never did understand the meaning of the words

"Socialism," "Communism," "the working class"—the words most often repeated—we younger children thought these words the most dangerous for our goats. We cried because of these words and went down to the cellar and out into the courtyard to assure ourselves that our goats were still there; we would bring them upstairs with us, into our rooms, and hide them in the cabinets in which Father kept his old books.

First we brought Stalinka, the most threatened, and then the other goats as well. From the radio, the speaker's wretched voice continued to blast: "Let the goats be destroyed! May the land be saved! Onward into the new five-year plan without goats . . ."

My brother the party member, godfather to our Stalinka, was glued to the peacock radio, and he tried to explain these unknown words to us, to calm us, but he had the opposite effect. We understood less and less of what he was saying.

The younger children's crying did not subside.

The goats proudly walked about the room.

The speaker's voice did not let up: "When we destroy the goats, our fields and our hills will bloom. Energy like we have never seen will be liberated; we will turn the earth into a garden of paradise.

"Millions of goatherds across the country will become a steely, defiant working class. They will build great factories; miners will dig deep into the earth . . ."

The radio resounded forcefully. The goats now moved about the rooms in fright. We hadn't noticed when Father came home. He was usually at work at this time. Our tearful eyes turned toward him. As always when things were hard for us in life, we waited for comfort from his tender gaze, from the blessed blueness of his eyes, which calmed us, pulled us away from difficult times. My father knew all the secrets of the family and of the goats. His presence always calmed us.

He turned down the volume on the radio, the goats settled down, and we continued listening to the speaker's voice: "Goatherds, come to your senses before it is too late; leave your goats. Tractors, bulldozers, combines, and locomotives await you! Are you going to work these machines with your goats? As your ancestors used to say, you don't even plow the fields with goats . . ."

Mother sensed my father's return. In a moment, she was there with us. She, too, had felt the blows of fate deep in her soul. She joined us in listening to the radio as the same voice continued: "Goatherds young and old, mothers and children, our invincible party finds itself facing yet another enemy. Our glorious party has successfully led the people in the battle against Fascism and will easily cope with the goats, those white devils, which our class enemy uses for himself. We have taken away their lands, their stores, they have nothing except their evil spirit, and, understandably, the goats have become their friends . . ."

My father listened with concern to the voice on the radio. Though he tried to hide his anxiety from us children, his eyes did not hold that blue tranquility in which our frightened thoughts often sailed away.

My father foresaw strict measures. Many more words, equally painful, equally vague, came from the radio, that cursed machine that, like fate's double, warned our family about the past and the future.

The speaker continued: "Friends, men and women, villagers, young men and women, a great nationwide action stands before us. The class enemy lifts his head too high. We must cut it off. We organize cooperatives, and they boycott them; we create collectives, they seek to own their private stores. But our party has glorious experience, and in the end, we will triumph; we will defeat the goats . . . We appeal to all of you to understand our actions correctly. Free yourselves from the goats to save us time and resources. The party is on your side; it has great revolutionary experience and can destroy every enemy, whoever it may be . . ."

As we listened to the radio, we did not take our eyes off our father. His face now brightened; the clear blue returned to his eyes and calmed us. It was obvious that the overblown aggression broadcast from the radio emitted powerlessness as well. My father most feared unexpected blows of fate. When those blows could be predicted, there was time to meet them prepared. Therefore he was calm, no matter how menacing the voice on the radio seemed to all of us.

"The plan for the destruction of the goats has been worked out to its finest detail at the highest levels of party government, at both the republic and federal levels.

"There, no mistake is ever made. The higher, the brighter, in the spirit of our new party consciousness. In our city we are the most affected by the goats. What sort of capital city has goats and, at its center, a Goatherd Quarter—that cursed nest of the white counterrevolution? Just think, there are families there with three to five goats, and there are goatherds, fanatics, with entire herds . . ."

For the first time, Father commented on the speaker's words at the moment he mentioned the goats in the Goatherd Quarter. "That's because here in the Goatherd Quarter live the poorest people; that's why there are the most goats here."

But who would listen to my father? The speaker, with heightened intonation and raised voice, said, "Comrades, the enemy must not catch us sleeping. The party has already adopted a strict position for its future actions against the goats; directives have been given. The National Assembly, after quick action, will adopt the Law Prohibiting the Keeping of Goats. The National Front must now begin its necessary work to educate the people.

"Death to the goats, freedom to the people!"

Finally, the toxic voice on the radio that embittered the lives of every family in the Goatherd Quarter quieted down.

Now came revolutionary songs of the masses. As the first chords struck, my father turned off the radio. It was enough for one day, too much, really.

The first thing he usually did to lessen the tension among us, to show that we were not on the verge of some bad luck, was to ask my mother about some routine household matters.

We ran to our goats. With tears in our eyes, we hugged them as if we were being parted from them forever. Who could enter our souls and the souls of these young, tender creatures with such serenity in their expression, so much sympathy for our poverty in this restless, uncertain, cursed Balkan time?

We, too, were a part of the white matter that, during the critical time when we were born and raised, had poured into us through an invisible stream of milk.

Now they wanted to separate us from our goats, from our very selves.

Could there be a greater Balkan curse than this?

Why must Stalinism toy so much with our souls in order to build Communism?

Why did they have to plant these untested ideas so deeply here where we lived?

Most of all, we hugged and fussed over our Stalinka because of the unforeseen change in relations between our country and Stalin. She would surely be the first to be taken away.

My father had stepped out of his usual daily rhythm. We followed his movements. Even when there were deaths in the family, his movements and his expression had not been so altered. His eyes reflected his soul, and now they surely radiated his despair as well. He looked through them now at our collective misfortune. No matter how much we were consoled by Mother's maxim—shared misfortune was less misfortune—death was clearly knocking at our door. This time, it had come calling for the family, for the Goatherd Quarter. My father, in his nervousness, turned back to the radio. He wanted to be fully immersed in the course of events. Now from the radio another voice resounded: "Comrades, members of the working class, and peasants, you have heard the announcement of the Central Committee of the Communist Party of Yugoslavia. Now we are alone in the ocean of Communism. Tighten your ranks. Stalin has excluded us from the Socialist Union. He wanted to subjugate our glorious party, which was hardened in our great battles in the war against Fascism. He wants to turn us into slaves, but we did not betray ourselves. Our leader, who led us in the National Liberation War, has won the final battle to save our country."

The radio seemed to sow terror in this house that had for years radiated calm. How was it possible for so much history to gather, thicken, and spread all in one day? And yet, the history of the Balkans has always been like this; it comes and goes in a blizzard, stays a frozen mass in the soul of the people, and thaws with difficulty. It was as if the radio had gone mad. For years my father had kept the voice of the radio from our ears and our mother's lest it sow too much unease in our souls. He wanted first to filter this heavy-handed propaganda, which always aimed to shape the souls of the people as if with a hammer. This time, the order of events in our house was lost, and each one of us had to pay the price through new outbursts of anxiety.

We were even more frightened by the speaker's latest words concerning the break with Stalin. We went, of course, once again to our Stalinka. We now knew that there was no salvation for her. The poor thing would suffer no matter what. Had we remained on good terms with Stalin, we would have been charged with mocking the name of the glorious Stalin; now, with our quarrels with Stalin, we would remain hardcore Stalinists. Now we all hugged our Stalinka as if we wanted her to understand that we would never get over mourning her, our great rescuer, who was certain to become the first victim of Stalinism in this southern part of the Balkans.

Revolutionary songs now boomed from the radio:

Yugoslavia, your people celebrate you . . . With Marshall Tito, our heroic son, not even hell can stop us.

Hell was sure to come. Poor us, poor goats. Our shared time. Our shared time was going to be taken from us.

New revolutionary songs followed . . .

My father turned off the radio, unplugged the cord, and went to his room with the radio—that demented apparatus—which had, in such a short time, sown so much unease. The old well-known quiet, as quiet as the bottom of the sea, set to the rhythm of our flowing tears, returned to our house.

We went with Stalinka and our other goats to the river as if we wanted to verify this latest turn in the course of history. The river flowed as always, and the shadow of the tall poplars played on the green-blue water of the river.

We set off together toward the willow grove by the river's edge, to the succulent leaves and clear waters. As if by some prior friendly agreement, the goatherds had also set off toward the river with the neighborhood goats, all moving in the current of these latest historical events.

The waters of the river, shimmering from blue to green, welcomed this white current on their banks, as seagulls were flying in from the southern sea. These were the last moments in our childhood paradise with the goats.

16

*W*hen we wanted to see the most beautiful and biggest snowfall of our lives, we looked back, deep into our childhood, to the time of the goats. In the city where we were raised and planted lifelong roots, the truly great snows vanished forever. And even, if after many, many years, a big snowfall did come, it would quickly become dirty and lose its beauty. It was slow to melt, holding the city for a long time frozen, enslaved . . .

The big snowfalls of our childhood turned the city white as in fairy tales; it was magical. First to cut their way through were the old horse-drawn carriages brought here at the turn of the century. In the court-yards, icicles clinging to the small fountains created small palaces, and fortresses like nothing you've ever seen before in your life.

Then we stepped out into the whiteness with our goats. They were white like the snow, their eyes sparkling, and they shone like small suns warming our childhood. We could not have imagined, not even in our dreams, that this was the last winter of our time of the goats. Stormy events came to our country after the conflict with Stalin and the consequences that followed: our country's increased isolation, then the intense hunger, followed by those unforgettable packages from America (we never forgot the sweetened canned meat, the powdered milk and eggs), then the border incidents and the first victims of border conflicts with our neighboring Socialist countries. At long last, the Law Prohibiting the Keeping of Goats was introduced, but it had still not been published in the country's official newspaper, the first step toward putting the law into effect. The destructive avalanche came at the time of this big, beautiful, silvery snowfall.

People did not let go of their fear, just as on the eve of war. The fear they had suffered in the most recent war—with its victims, camps, and deportations—had still not abated, but already a new reality was setting in: fear aroused by the war against the goats. The law was strict; it could not have been stricter. The goats were to be liquidated, period. If the owners of the goats did not carry out this order, troikas, specially trained teams of three, would come. And then: the knife. All that remained was to choose the means of death. But what sort of people could imagine raising a knife against their goats, against themselves?

The quarrel with Stalin left us little time and little hope that the goats would remain alive. We thought we had been freed of Stalinism forever, but it remained within us for a long, long time, and in some people, it had taken root forever. It was most important for us that our goats stay alive as long as possible, even if it meant making our peace with Stalin and confessing to him "our errors." And so it was, after the great quarrel between Tito and Stalin, spring or summer, fall or winter, that we always felt that we were walking our goats for the last time. We knew that the wolf was at our heels, as in the fable of Mr. Seguin's goat. The wolf was always here, but our goats were not alone. We promised them that we would protect them with our lives if necessary. As for them, poor things, they did not voice approval or opposition. They simply searched out the next blade of grass—our future life-saving drop of milk.

When the prohibition against keeping goats had been approved but the law was not yet in force, we brought our goats everywhere, even to school. If they were going to be taken, let them be taken from us while we were with them. On the day of the big snowfall, we barely got to school ourselves. We begged our parents to guard the goats for us until we returned. In the courtyard of the school, there was not the usual commotion; there couldn't be, because of all the snow. There had been snow in other years, but the school had been unable to stop the children's rough-and-tumble play. Had something happened? Our hearts pounded.

Our teacher had three children and a goat named Mila, or Sweetheart. She was always in front of the school, there by the teacher's house, regardless of the time of year. When we grazed our goats, we took Mila along. We took turns taking her because we all wanted to have her with us, not only because of the teacher, but also because of his young children, who had been left motherless at an early age. When the time came, we even took Mila to Changa. She was like our own goat.

But look! For the first time, she was not there in front of the school! Maybe, because of the snow, she's in some other spot, we thought, consoling ourselves. But that was not the case . . .

Our teacher was standing alone in the doorway to the school. Without our asking, he told us that Mila was alive and would return. The teacher's sad-faced children were there as well. We all knew, without a doubt, that Mila had saved the teacher's children from certain death after their mother died.

"Where's Mila?" we asked, but what had happened to her we only understood later, or, more accurately, we never really understood.

Before Mila's disappearance, our teacher had been charged with keeping goats illegally. There had been a few warnings circulating, especially from the parents of the schoolchildren, for the teacher to get rid of his goat, but he would not part with Mila. His family could not survive without her. Had the teacher been a member of the party, he might have been charged later. As it was, Mila was among the first on the list for liquidation because the teacher had raised the ire of a number of people by keeping a goat on the very doorstep of the school.

The governmental powers and the party had a clear strategy: they would start by liquidating the goats of a certain number of intellectuals, leaders in public and cultural life, and then it would surely be easier later on to deal with the simple goatherds.

The teacher was indicted and was within the reach of the law. At that time, if they had you in their sights, they would strike. You never knew who was firing or why: some for personal reasons, others on account of the goats, others to advance their careers. The teacher understood: first indictment, then trial, and then the knife for the goat and jail for him. He had no choice.

One morning, after the big snowfall, right at the crack of dawn, the teacher took Mila and headed to the mountains. It was as if he were reenacting, along some unknown path, a Balkan variation of the death of Mr. Seguin's goat.

Here, as in the other story, there was a wolf, but it was not clear which wolf was the real one, because there was more than one.

Mila set off along her path. She peacefully accepted this uncertain, unanticipated trip along the ridges and up to the mountain crest, to a rustling meadow and a lonely hut. There, forgotten by everyone, lived an extremely poor family: an old man and old woman with their goat; their children had long since left to find work abroad and had not been heard from for years.

When he had first discovered these mountain recluses, the teacher began to love them like his own family. He went three times a year and brought them warm clothing, food, sugar, and salt. These old people, who had been attached to this mountain for so many years and were now unable to come down into the valley, accepted Mila as their child. "Just for a short time," the teacher told them, though he himself did not know how long that time would be. He hoped that some way would be found so that the time of the goats could continue. But until then, the old folks could live for a while with the goats, thanks to the goats. And if that hoped-for time never came, they would remain free in the mountain. Perhaps wild animals would devour them, too—wolves most likely—just like the little goat of Mr. Seguin. The teacher was happy that Mila and the other goats would not be slain by some knife-wielding ingrate.

The teacher never returned from the mountain. Surely, his way had been blocked by a blizzard. An avalanche, perhaps. No one ever knew what happened on his way back. People from the court arrived to carry out the charges. The teacher was not there; only his children were. We gave them food and brought them milk and bread for porridge. People from the court questioned us, too. We recognized the official from the census commission. They asked us where the teacher and Mila were hiding. They made us take them to the places where we had led Mila and our goats to pasture. They frightened us by saying that we would be sent to a juvenile detention center since we were too young for prison. They finally concluded that we did not know anything. They sent search parties through the mountains. They did not find the teacher. He did not return in the spring after the snow melted. His children were placed in foster homes; we never saw them again, nor the teacher, nor Mila.

After we had grown up, whenever a snowstorm came, we searched the snow to discover traces of the hooves left by the little goat Mila, who was surely looking for the teacher and his children, for all of us in the time of the goats.

17

A terrible fear gripped the Goatherd Quarter after the first news of the prohibition against the goats. This fear became even greater when word got around that Changa had vanished with his huge herd of goats. Nearly every family had a plan for saving its goats. Our family was concerned about Changa's disappearance as well as the fate of our goats.

Everyone asked where Changa was, where his goats were. Everyone had a theory as to what had happened. The party spread rumors that Changa had betrayed them and handed himself and the goats over to those in power. According to others, Changa had fled across the border with the goats. Several malicious people said privately that he was a spy who had worked constantly with the government in the Goatherd Quarter and now had left everyone in the lurch. No one believed these rumors, but until Changa appeared with the goats, it was impossible to disprove them. It was a sad time in the Goatherd Quarter and in the city without Changa, without his does and bucks. We all waited for his return. He had to return.

Changa simply could not make peace with the Socialism that was destroying the goats. After many conversations with my father and with other respected goatherds in the city, Changa decided to go to the leaders of the federal government, to go to the central powers of the country, and, if necessary, to have a discussion with the main strategist in charge of the goat question; he even dreamed of visiting the Leader himself. My father tried to stop him; he told him that he would never reach those key people; he would be lost in the web spun by the lower functionaries.

Changa usually followed through on his intentions; no force could stop him, especially when his instinct led him to the truth. In one of their last conversations, my father suggested that the person most responsible for the goat question was likely outside of the country. Changa knew quite well that Father was thinking of Stalin and had even said to him once, "I will do whatever it takes to discover the truth about the goats. I will even go see Stalin. I must save the goats!"

My father had shaken his head doubtfully. This was a time when a person did not even dare mention the name of Stalin, let alone contemplate going to see him.

Changa had important, incredible connections everywhere, even in some countries to the east of us, where the goat question was being discussed. According to Changa, the Cominform, the central Communist organization, had discussed the goat question from the beginning and had decided that no single policy would be put into effect; rather, each individual party would be left to resolve it according to conditions in each country.

In our country, Changa reasoned, the conditions for building Socialism were unique, and, therefore, the goat question had to be solved the right way. But the fact that our country comprised separate republics—nothing here was ever straightforward—caused him to hesitate a bit in following this train of thought.

My father had seen all kinds of strange things in the Balkans, but for him what was happening with the goats was the strangest and most incredible of all. At the beginning of the century, he had lived through the fall of the Ottoman Empire and had scraped through the Balkan wars, followed by the First and Second World Wars, but until now no one had laid a finger on the goats. The century went by with them. And why would anyone touch them, when, through all the wars, the goats had not bothered the victors or the vanquished. They had served everyone loyally. In the Balkans, nothing endured, except, of course, the goats! But now the party was destroying them, too. Cursed times.

People predicted that tragic events would unfold in the Goatherd Quarter without Changa. People began to hide their goats. In the courtyards of their homes, they dug underground rooms, bunkers, to live in; it was as if every house had become its own small fortress. As if everyone were waiting for the Apocalypse.

But one morning, the Good Lord woke the people in the Goatherd Quarter.

"Changa's back!"

"He's back! Changa!"

His song echoed through the city, just like the songs of the revolutionaries and the victors that had resounded before. The goats also came flying in. And when we awoke, we did not know whether we were returning to sleep or dreaming a new dream. After a long absence, clouds of dust from the hooves of the goats once again hung above the city streets. The hustle and bustle of life returned from all sides.

"Changa is back!" "Long live Changa!" "Long live the goats!" "Tito—Changa!" was heard in all directions, just as it was during the time when people shouted, "Tito—Stalin!"

The goats stepped out and joined ranks with the goatherds behind Changa's famous herd; it was like the great May Day parades. Our great savior had returned from points unknown. The mothers compared him with God; we, with Stalin, in private, of course, thinking that since his picture had disappeared from its place alongside Tito's, we needed another Stalin. Poor things that we were, we could not get by for long without Stalin. Changa could be our new Stalin. He would be the protector of our goats and of our lives. The brave, the illiterate, and the poorly informed among us shouted out "Changa—Stalin!" without being aware of the danger. Some people even went so far as to put up posters, hand out leaflets, and display banners with slogans in favor of the goats and extolling their virtues. One encountered posters expressing every point of view: "Long live your neighbor's goat!" "Together with the goats toward new victories of the working class!" "Death to the goats, freedom to the people!"

Changa quickly found himself in the middle of the square surrounded by thousands of people and goats. The ruling powers—the party and the police—were perturbed. No one but Changa was prepared for such a turn of events in the city. Telegrams quickly traveled along the wires to the highest levels of command, seeking quick instructions before this "white revolution" could spread. In a day or two the Law Prohibiting the Keeping of Goats was to come into effect. The ruling powers still had no instructions, could take no initiative. The law could not be put into effect unless it were done illegally. In the meantime, the local authorities had to decide for themselves what to do to stop Changa and the goats. But it was not easy for them; the whole city was now with Changa.

Everyone in the square waited for Changa; on the viewing stand sat representatives of the government and the municipal party just as on the day when Changa had come to the city with the goats and the goatherds, when they had stopped here. Since then, a lot of water had flowed under the bridge. At that time, he and the goatherds had been greeted with bread and salt; he had been given a roof over his head. There had even been a certain understanding about the goats. Yet even then, the government and the party had had their doubts.

It was already more than clear: the goatherds had not become the working class. The great ideals of the party and the builders of Socialism had failed. The goatherds had not abandoned their goats. They had not become a working class, but their children had grown and were the future of the country. But what if there had been no goats?

Changa delivered an important speech. He was witness to the time of the goats from its beginning until today. He was well prepared. He knew that his words would soon be typed up and sent off to the republic and federal governments as well as to the party leadership, and so he left nothing unspoken. He had clearly conquered his fear; now he wanted to free all the goatherds, young and old . . .

My father was not in the square. He had not known about the event. He had some urgent business in the court. Had he known about Changa's return and the assembly in the square, he would surely have put aside all his other obligations. He was visibly worried—there had been no news of Changa for a long time. And now, today's big news had caught him unprepared! He could barely believe it when we came back from the meeting and told him the news as we entered the house together with our three goats. With concern, he patted our heads; his face broke into that smile that always gave us the courage to hold on to our hope.

All of us, both young and old, knew about the recent news on the radio, about Stalin's threats and the attacks on the goats; all of us waited for the last judgment against the goats, the end of the time of the goats. We lived in this moment of newfound luck. That is how our family's whole life had been. Yes, we allowed ourselves to live in happiness, until the unhappy end of the goats would seize us; we did not want to relinquish our last moments of happiness with them.

When Mother saw us all together with our goats, she greeted us calmly at the door. Her face was illuminated by the expression that adorned her face whenever we were all together. She had endless questions she wanted to ask us, but she remained silent. Were they going to take the goats away and kill them? Was it true that the goats were being killed en masse with machine guns and cannon fire in the other republics? Were the goatherds being imprisoned, or indicted, or deported?

Life had taught my father not to give in to misfortune prematurely but to use the time remaining to think how to use his strengths to oppose it.

"Changa has returned, so surely better days are coming for the goats," my mother said, breaking the silence.

We had been waiting impatiently to start a conversation about Changa and the goats.

"Changa has returned," my father agreed, "but the problem with the goats remains. These are now the most difficult times; one has to be careful . . ."

His reproach was almost imperceptibly directed toward my mother. She had let us go out with our goats.

"All the goats from the neighborhood were out with the children and goatherds, so I figured . . ." she said gently.

"Yes, yes, everyone was out with the goats," we all concurred in unison.

"That's fine, you all did the right thing," my father continued. "But be careful in the future. The wolf does not rest while it watches the goats. Even without the goats, we will be among the first attacked!"

For the first time, my father was both categorical and clear about our fate and the fate of the goats. But Mother, naturally, wanted to calm us, so she spoke to my father in a different tone: "Surely Changa has good news!"

She was returning to her original thought.

My father did not say anything more, but he had much to tell. His silence spoke more than words. He left us with our thoughts.

He knew Changa's big soul very well. The bond of trust between them seemed to meld their souls during those critical times in their battles for survival, in these entangled Balkan times when impatience to reach peaceful solutions more often led to the drawing of a knife. He clearly felt that Changa had reached the brink of despair. Of course, there was not, nor could there be, good news (an answer he owed my mother), so he tried to do what he could not.

After we had eaten dinner in silence, my father went off to his study for his customary repose. He stayed there a long time. Surely he was waiting for Changa.

Time passed slowly. While we were waiting, it seemed to us that even the river was flowing more slowly. The quiet wind blowing from the river rustled the smooth leaves of the mammoth poplars that had grown in solitude for so many years opposite the fortress as if they had decided to surpass its height. Thousands of jackdaws flew out from the crevices in the fortress walls. With their melancholy flight and common cry, they seemed to defend the blueness of the sky and conjure up distant and unknown travels. They settled in the branches of the poplars. When they flew in a great flock, they covered the river like a black cloud. The jackdaws' flight across the river was a part of the landscape we sometimes interpreted as a sign of misfortune. Our childish voices would then call out as if we wanted to drown out the jackdaws hidden in the crowns of the great poplars, in the cavities time had worn in the fortress walls or on the large stone columns. But now the flight of the jackdaws from the fortress seemed to drown out our childhood cries even before they sounded. For the first time, the cries of the black birds were the only sounds around; they cut the silence, sharply and forebodingly.

The Goatherd Quarter was sinking into a restless dream. All our dreams were different, but in all of them our goats were the great heroes. We were somewhere between dream and reality. We were waiting for Changa. We were awake when the familiar ring of the front doorbell sounded. My mother got there first to open it.

Changa charged up the stairs to Father's room with rapid steps. The old yellow light was shining above the open books. Everything was as it always was, ready for travel along the waves of time, along the pages of the opened books.

My mother came into the room where we slept, though we were now awake, to cover us, to cover us with care. She moved silently, even though she knew we were not sleeping. We, in turn, knew that she would not close an eye as long as the golden lamp shone in Father's study. It was as if we had some kind of sacred pact with the quiet of the old house. Not only did we catch the sound of every rustle in the quietness, but we interpreted it more clearly than the sounds of the flowing river.

During those gentle, quiet nights when the weather was pleasant, my mother would open all the large windows, and we could even hear the breathing of the river that so vividly connected us with the flow of time. The river entered our dreams and changed them. Now more clearly than ever we heard the quiet sound of the poplar leaves beside the waters of the river.

My father greeted Changa calmly as he turned a fresh page of his open book. Right away, the goatherd drank in Father's calm, which came most likely from his eternal reading. Here, in full view of Father's books, he wanted to pour out all the words pent up inside him, all the things he had layered in his soul ever since the time they had last been together. Here, in this quiet fortress of books from every era, he wanted to regain his former calm. Rage and tranquility, anger and kindness, sorrow and joy, power and powerlessness were so intertwined within him that it was difficult for him to separate them. Perhaps this is what drew him so close to my father. In Father's presence, no matter what he said, no matter what burst forth from his soul, he always remained himself—Changa. If, when he was with others, as he so often was, he were to unburden the things weighing on his soul, there would surely have been endless quarrels and confrontations. It was the same for my father. When he was with Changa, no matter how much he poured from his soul, he remained himself.

After they had sat in silence a moment, a custom established from their earlier meetings, Changa spoke first: "Hard times are coming; it's hard to know what tomorrow will bring."

"Hard times, hard times, indeed," my father agreed. "In the Balkans, good times have almost never lasted long. It was generally the rule that a little peace and good fortune were paid for with unpredictable tragic events. We never know when things will be better for us; the devil is always here, even when we find it difficult to detect him. You've been gone a long time, haven't you?" Father asked Changa.

"I was traveling. I even went to other republics."

"What is happening there? How did you travel? Where did you go?"

"I traveled the whole country on foot, by trains, and on trucks. I went different ways to different places. I was in the other republics—

goatherd republics, some more, some less. I even secretly crossed the border, trying to track down the truth about the goats. In other countries to the east, those that were until recently our friends and brothers, the highest levels of government are also trying to solve the goat problem."

Changa's words surprised my father. He had not believed that the goat question would be so entwined with politics and would be "internationalized." And he was dying to know what was happening in the other "goat republics" of Yugoslavia. There was much information from the Western radio stations, but now he could verify the news with first-hand information.

As if he could read my father's thoughts, Changa continued: "In the goat republics, terrible things are happening to the people and to their goats. I saw houses draped in black, mourning the death of people and goats! The land is as dry as the nursing mothers' breasts. Children are suffering. In destroying the goats, old accounts are being settled not just from the past war but from other wars as well. New powers are imposing a new order. The goats are being blamed for everything! It seems that Socialism always has to have some enemy for it to continue, and now it's the goats' turn! The nannies are now the main culprits. Before it was only the billies that were sacrificed . . ."

Changa's unpredictable train of thought trailed off, even though my father had not interrupted him. After a short silence, Changa again asked his old question: "Why are they killing the goats? What is this goat-fratricidal war all about?"

My father had no direct answer. Even had he tried to find an answer, he would not have been able to, because such an answer did not exist. It seemed to him an unusual turn of phrase: "goat-fratricidal war." Likely Changa was concealing there some unspoken significance. But in all likelihood it was connected with events Changa had witnessed. Changa continued: "Every republic had its own strategy for destroying the goats, worked out according to the general directive of the federation. And every district had to work out its own tactics. Who can make sense of this?

"There were special instructions for the ethnically and religiously mixed republics. There, they expected strong reactions, riots. There is not a single house that has not had a goat destroyed. In the republic in the middle of the country, the one considered the most mixed, the day of reckoning with the goats and goatherds had been most brutal. There, they told me about an unbelievable event, unique in the Yugoslav history of the liquidation of the goats . . . There was a family with three children and seventeen goats. When the prohibition came into effect, that family was to be the first target. Seventeen goats! Members of the commission came, and each day one goat was killed. The poor goatherd hid them, but, in the end, he could not keep them hidden. The government had precise numbers from the last goat census. According to their data, there were sixteen goats. One of the goats had had a kid after that census.

"The family of the poor goatherd were left with sixteen wounds in their souls. The census takers, damn them all, appeared the sixteenth day. They killed the last goat and left. Of course, they were working with the census lists. The old goatherd was left with the hidden buck. In principle, going by the census lists, the liquidation of the goats had been carried out to the letter, fine, but the goatherd knew that those wretches would come again to double check.

"During the night, the goatherd kept thinking what he could do. Should he flee from what was written? No, you can't escape fate. A thousand thoughts coursed through his head. Finally, an idea came to him! He had the skin of a lamb that had just been slaughtered, so he decided to sew it onto the goat. He and his wife, together with their hungry children, worked through the night, sewing on the skin. By morning, the goat had become a lamb!

"The first knock on the door comes; it's the census takers!

"They're back for one final check, even though, according to their census lists, everything was clear, more than clear. They look around, check everywhere, they stop by the goat turned lamb, they take a good look, they even hug it. No problem, a beautiful lamb, they said.

"They get ready to go. But just as the census team is about to leave, the 'lamb,' curse it, bleats like every other little kid . . .

112

"They turned around. The chief of police grabbed the 'lamb' with both hands. He lifted it off the ground high in the air. It bleated more loudly. The skin came unstitched, and out fell the kid. All hell descended on the house. They took away the old goatherd together with the goat. And another house was draped in black . . ."

Changa told this story with tears in his eyes. My father must have cried as well. There were other tragic incidents in that republic in the middle of the country. The incidents went from black to blacker; they were unthinkable. At the end, like a refrain to all he had narrated, Changa asked the question again, "Why are they killing the goats?"

My father was visibly upset by the incidents Changa had related to him. They caused him to think even more intently. But he was no closer to the answer Changa was seeking. Perhaps there was no true answer.

My father searched for an answer to the question of why they were killing the goats in a kind of Balkan vicious circle, in which one always returned to the beginning, a Balkan variation of the absurd. But why torment Changa now with his thoughts about the absurd when life itself was speaking?

My father thought a long time, especially after Changa had left, trying to discern the truth as to why the goats were being killed. He searched his trusted sources, but the more he read (especially about goats), the further he was from real-life answers. The great hostility these people demonstrated toward the goats was, in fact, directed toward themselves. As he delved to the bottom of ideas in his books about goats and the history of the "Third Empire," my father, thinking aloud, said, "Now in the empire of Stalinism, instead of sacrificing the 'lead buck,' they are killing the goats . . ."

"Yes," Changa would agree, "they are killing the goats!"

Changa's natural and powerful mind appealed to my father. He always focused on what was most vital. He had a powerful inner current that flowed toward truth and reality, drawing from the natural springs of life. And he had clear exits from the traps of various *isms*.

The route Changa followed toward the truth was usually not the one my father took. But their thoughts most often converged in a common goal. My father was patient in his conversations with the goat-herd; he did not want to wound a single atom of his great soul.

Changa had gathered additional information from the more developed northern republics and from the less developed central and southern republics concerning the fate of the goats and the goatherds. He had learned that one of the most intelligent men in Yugoslavia's supreme leadership—one who, like my father, read a great deal and whom the Leader himself most trusted, as had Stalin once upon a time—while engaged in the cultivation and discovery of mushrooms, especially in his native northern republic, had come up with the idea of ridding the country of goats and turning the land into gardens abounding in mush-rooms! He had firm faith in this plan and had convinced some other like-minded people, the majority of whom, of course, hailed from the northern republics. Together, they decided that the people of the southern republic should be transformed from herders, mountain people, and stockbreeders into a hard, steely, industrial working power of granite and steel—*the working class*. In the name of this future working class many things were carried out . . .

Later, as my father continued his study based on Changa's firsthand reports, he considered the Balkan misfortunes more broadly, especially during the time of the goats. He was sickened by the degree to which the goat question, a new offspring of Stalinism, had taken over the party ranks, those in power. Fanatic belief in the party easily turned into bloodthirstiness toward the goats, our childhoods. Were they so blinded that they could not see the consequences of killing the goats? They wanted to remain faithful to something indefinite that was not even an ideal. If it had been, at least there would have been some chance of a change in thinking, a chance of some hope.

Prompted by his search for an answer to Changa's question of why the goats were being killed, my father was prepared to write a new chapter in the book he was contemplating about the history of Balkan empires through the history of their collapse. This new chapter would be related to the myth of Balkan self-destruction, a syndrome of liquidations from which not a single Balkan nation had escaped. He was fascinated by the myth of the young mother who was sealed into the foundations of a bridge being built in Scutari, on the Bojana River, as well as other myths involving tragedies occurring during building and destruction. He then wanted to interpret the destruction of the goats through other Balkan myths as well, but Changa's interest stopped there.

Was it possible, he confided in Changa in carefully chosen words, for there to be a greater curse, a sacrifice more incomprehensible, than to build something, to raise it up, then knock it down and destroy it?

Changa, of course, always thought how the goats had been raised for centuries but were now being destroyed. My father thought of Changa as a cursed Balkan Sisyphus who struggles on behalf of the goats, those white stones condemned to perpetual destruction. That is how it has been for centuries in the Balkans: destroy and rebuild!

Even now, liberated after the victory over Fascism, it was necessary to pay a price, to destroy the goats—sacrifices to the absurd—the key to survival for the people living in the rocky relief of these unpredictable Balkan lands for centuries. Why, in the history of the Balkans, was it necessary to pay this goat tribute as well?

Why did these new victors strike at the goat, that animal sacred to the Balkans' poor? Not without reason has the strongest Balkan curse remained, "Death to your neighbor's goat!" But in whose name did the goats now need to die?

18

*I*t was as if the city were under occupation due to the unexpected appearance of Changa and the goats. The authorities and the party were at first confused, but they swiftly got organized. Instructions from the republic and federal parties arrived in short order. They left Changa to play out his swan song. He would draw together all the goats and goat-herds, who had until now been successfully hidden, and then they would all be captured.

Changa recalled Father telling him how each Balkan empire, from the Roman to the Byzantine and Ottoman, kept power for centuries by means of several basic strategies that were constantly renewed: "First divide, then conquer!"

And there were the Janissaries with their ultimate strategy: "Let them raise their heads, then cut them off!" My father had boundless love and respect for Changa; he was the friend of his life. More than anything in the world, he did not want something bad to happen to him. He feared most—and it was closest to the truth: Changa had been given a certain period to frolic about the city with the goats and in a triumphal march, to assemble the like-minded people, innocent members of the goat "working class." Then would come the end, once and for all, to the goat question under Socialism.

The cultivation of goats was, for my father, one of the most remarkable phenomena in human evolution. Man had to return to man his lost nature, beyond the boundaries of humankind. To cultivate goats meant to protect these mute, powerless creatures God had created and sent to man so he could protect himself with their help. My father believed that Changa was a kind of savior whose existence now hung in the balance between holy sacrifice and continued life.

Unlike my father, who learned more about real life through his collection of books, Changa experienced life through direct confrontation with it. This was the only way they could become so close to each other, keep alive the goat question, and create such strong bonds among the different groups of people in the Balkans, something the faiths and ideologies of past empires had not accomplished. They were united by their shared experience of suffering the vicissitudes of life. Changa's wish was often taken up by my father, and my father's ideas often helped shape Changa's wish. Fortunately, they complemented each other yet preserved their autonomy.

As prince of the goats, Changa commanded the city.

The goats accompanied him like a host of light, white angels. The people in the Goatherd Quarter, like everyone else in the city with goats, had painful experiences with the goat commissions: some had had their goats brazenly taken away; other families had their goats slaughtered before their eyes; still others were taken with their goats to court. But not all the goats had been destroyed, nor were they all documented. Goats began to appear as if they were materializing from the ground to join Changa and his frolicking herd in the city. Yes, there were some lucky folk who survived each circle of hell created by those all-powerful commissions; they had saved their goats for this day alone and for the resurrection of Changa's herd. The surviving goats in the city joined with the goats that had fled with Changa and now marched through the great square. It was lively and solemn, reminiscent of great May Day celebrations or a military parade.

People with fresh memories of the recent traumatic events came out of their houses to greet Changa, with renewed hope that the time of the goats would return. But there were those who sensed that Changa and the goats were marching straight to their deaths.

Vigilant hidden eyes followed Changa's movements.

D-day had been set for the final reckoning with Changa and his goats, with all the goats of the city, with all the goats of our time. Every bit of information about Changa's comings and goings with the goats was gathered in a single central location.

In the other republics, the goat question had already been "resolved" or was nearing its denouement. There were precise reports from even the most remote mountain villages, from the cities, from the valleys, concerning the liquidation of thousands and thousands of goats.

The Communist strategists had precise data about the goatherds, the newly minted members of the working class who were needed to build the great factories, the roads, the bridges, the dams, and the hydro-electric stations.

Around the clock, reports reached the center concerning the goats' conduct, encrypted messages were sent to republic headquarters, descriptions of events were compiled, reports and directives were sent, and a plan was hatched for the final assault against the "white counterrevolution."

The city was surrounded by military and police forces. Roads leading from the city and the border crossings were under strict control. Instructions, posters, and warrants with pictures of Changa and his lead buck were printed. Rewards were promised. Everything had to be considered. After all, Changa could flee with a few does and a buck, hide them somewhere, and, in time, the goats would multiply and return once again to the city.

Everything had to be planned!

The gains of the revolution hung in the balance.

Socialism was threatened!

The goats could not just up and block the course of history, that inevitable march toward a new Socialist society, the working class its main guarantor! This "genetic mistake" must be corrected.

"It must, it must, it must!" echoed from all sides.

On the eve of D-day, Changa called together the goatherds, both veterans and young ones and those goatherds whose goats had been killed; he invited them to come with their families to the wild part of the large city park by the river to celebrate his return with the goats.

People were surprised.

Now what was Changa up to?

What kind of celebration could there be, when the noose was being readied and his days were numbered, both his and the goats'?

I remember one exchange between my father and Changa whose meaning has now become clearer to me. In conversation, my father had asked Changa, "Is there a hell?"

"There is!"

"Where is it?"

"Where all hope is lost!" Changa had answered.

In his conduct and bearing, the goatherd demonstrated that hope is an instinct destroyed only by thought. The goats, those creatures whose consciousness seemed to meld with his own, showed him that they do not know hopelessness. From them he drew strength to persevere.

People and goats hurried from every direction toward the river. Old folk, mothers with children, pregnant women. Everyone, all the people who owed their lives to the goats and to Changa. It seemed as if they were heading to the center of life, where they would build a dam to protect the river of life. No one could stop this movement of people and goats under Changa's command.

The authorities did not want to act precipitously. For the action to unfold as planned, several more hours of night had to pass. In the end, the goats would surely be flying toward the heavens.

The goatherds would be imprisoned. Not all, of course; the authorities would make an example of the most combative, the most resistant. Changa must be captured alive at all cost. An extensive trial would be arranged for him. They would invite representatives from all the republics; foreign observers would be allowed to attend. This would be a great display of judicial processes in the southern republic. Let the world understand the southern republic and its Socialist path. Why should these damned goatherds turn the course of history? Why should they caper about the earth with their goats? They shall build railroads; they shall raise bridges; they shall produce tractors and locomotives. Those damned goats, those white devils!

The white columns merged in a broad swath ending deep in the forest in an area hardly known to many of the goatherds. All the faithful goatherds had come, even from other cities. They had artfully slipped past the blockades around the city.

Changa greeted everyone. He was wearing a magnificent long goatskin cloak made from thousands of white shaggy fibers that shone like rays radiating from the goats' sun-king.

My father usually stayed clear of the goatherds' events. He wanted to be involved with the goatherds and their problems in a different manner. His involvement in goat matters was, in fact, principally through his friendship and cooperation with Changa. Everyone knew about their "goat coalition," about the bond between the intellectual and the goatherd forged in the crucial question of survival.

When we children were ready to go to the park, to the last big meeting with Changa and his goats, my father stopped us at the door and told us to wait for him because he wanted to come with us. We were surprised, but we were even more surprised when our mother also joined us.

My father never left the house without his hat; this time was no different. My mother suggested that perhaps he should make an exception and leave it at home. It did not seem right for him to appear among the goatherds with that hat! My father stuck to his custom, and my mother did not insist. We all set off together toward the goats.

As soon as he caught sight of my father and his hat from a distance, Changa could not believe his eyes. They warmly embraced. My mother greeted Changa with tears in her eyes. She had a premonition of something; we children could read it in her eyes.

Changa greeted everyone cheerfully. He had brought large barrels of goat cheese, which he divided among the people. For everyone there was a kind word; he remembered everyone's goats, even those now dead.

The city had never seen a more beautiful, more splendid celebration. Those holiday evenings with fireworks and cannon fire—Labor Day, May Day, the Day of Victory, the Day of the Army—all these sank into oblivion . . .

For us, the holiday of Changa and his goats was the most beautiful holiday in the world. After most other big holiday celebrations, a certain sadness and uncertainty descended on the city.

But who could imagine misfortune in this shared happiness between humans and goats? Oh, how many people had overcome the beast in them, and how many goats demonstrated their humanity! Those who cordoned off the city on all sides, curse them, had divided the people into classes, into allies and class enemies. They set one against the other! How could they understand these people standing with their goats? These goats standing with their people?

A song rang out. There were revolutionary tunes in which Stalin's name was replaced by Changa. The goats were inserted into the lyrics. Many songs were sung loudly on that happy night. The songs carried along the river; they reached the city and the square. Fireworks shot into the air. One, two, three—they exploded in bouquets of wondrous shades—blue, yellow, and red. The sky filled as if it were raining stars.

There were anxious people in the city. They could do nothing without instructions. And they could not get those right away. No one but

Changa could have supplied those fireworks. For us children they were better than the ones on May Day.

Night conquered the day. The sky was covered with dark clouds. The first drops of rain dripped through the leaves. People began to disperse. As the night grew shorter, one after another, everyone said good-bye to Changa. We were the last to say good-bye. Changa gave me, the youngest there, a knife with a goat-horn handle. He parted last with my father. They did not say a word to each other, but those are the moments in which the most is said. True friendship is a whisper of the soul; nothing can replace it. It can't be purchased; it comes of its own accord.

We left. Changa stayed behind alone. No, he was not alone. All the goats were with him. Several goats beside him had broad, smooth faces; they emitted sounds that were almost human. Without a doubt, they were humanlike animals.

When we returned home, my father continued reading long into the night. He could not turn out the golden lamp. My mother continued to invent new patterns for her knitting. We children thought of our goats and our times together. Now they were with Changa; only he could protect them, keep them, and save them from death. Only Changa was not afraid of death. Changa, the hero of our time of the goats.

19

A pearly day dawned above the fortress.

We parted from the dream we shared with our goats. D-day had set in. The last day with the goats and Changa. The end of the time of the goats.

D-day was wondrously beautiful. A gift of nature. There had never been a more beautiful day. A day worth a whole lifetime. As usual, my mother woke early to put the house in order, even though she had done so before going to bed. That's the way she closed the circle of day and night. As always, she set out into the courtyard to see the goats but gave a start when she remembered that the goats had been left with Changa's goats to share their common fate.

She went to the courtyard gate that opened onto the street, toward the river, toward the large poplars, toward the fortress. A large red fire engine racing toward the park blocked her view. She saw hundreds of police, soldiers dressed in strange, multicolored clothing holding big clubs and shields as they moved to the park. The people whom she usually met at this time—the newspaperman who stood on the corner at the head of the Wooden Bridge, the milkman—weren't in their customary places, nor were the other early risers. Only the chirping of birds reminded her of other, more ordinary days.

"This does not look good," my mother muttered and headed back toward the courtyard and the kitchen.

We were all awake, just as during the time of the goats. I, the sleepyhead, was last to drag myself up. My father was sitting at the head of the table waiting for his tea. Something had upset the usual order of things. My mother entered the house, her face pale. It took all her strength to suppress her concern. The character of her soul was reflected in her eyes, and we children clearly read her mood. Mother's language radiated from her eyes; here one could read what was written. Quietly, she told us what she had seen. She had never seen so many people in uniform, even during those times when she had been compelled to greet different soldiers at our house by the lake. These were different times, times of freedom, but nevertheless there were so many soldiers and police with clubs and shields. She could not understand what was going on. If it had not involved the fate of the goats, everything would have unfolded differently. My father tried to calm her, to turn the course of our anxious thoughts: "It is likely a military exercise. It will pass quickly. What hasn't passed through the Balkans?"

Father's words did not ease our fear. My mother slowly served the tea. She wanted to bring back the usual order to the day. My father then added that nothing was going to happen to the goats. But we children put two and two together. I started to cry, and soon my brothers were rushing to the door. Of course, they planned to go to the park, to reach the goats, to get past the columns of soldiers and policemen, to warn Changa and take our goats as well. My father stopped them. "Wait, children, calm down. Let us wait awhile. Do not be the first to go out!"

My father locked the courtyard gate tightly. We all returned to our places. My mother collected the untouched food. We moved about the house and the courtyard, closed in and powerless. We didn't have our goats. We paced like animals in a cage. My father did not even allow us to look out the window toward the quay that led to the park.

Finally, my oldest brother climbed into a tall mulberry tree, high enough to see the street, the quay, the Kale. The others climbed too. Our parents could not stop us.

The street was empty as never before at this time of day. From time to time, a red fire truck went past. There had been no fires in the city for years, and now, in the space of such a short time, so many fires? It was unbelievable. We waited silently in the tall tree trunk. We were tormented by terrible premonitions. Our neighbors, hidden, were also in the grip of uncertainty. One thought united us: What was happening to Changa and our goats? The empty trucks whizzing past heading to the park interrupted our thoughts. This intensified our fear. Surely, Changa and the goats had been killed, and now they were going to collect them with the trucks. We, poor things, were thinking mostly about our goats Brighty, Ugly, and Stalinka (now called Liberty). Our spirits froze. They had never been colder.

A knock at the door, first soft, then stronger, interrupted our anxiety. Mother reached the door first, just as she had during the war when soldiers had knocked at our door. Father wanted to hold her back, but she was already at the doorway. We quickly climbed down from the mulberry tree. My mother slowly opened the door. There were three people standing there. We immediately recognized the leader of the census takers who had come before, the man from the police, with his leather jacket and now an even bigger moustache, and that settled us a little. But next to him was a soldier with a machine gun trained at us and a third, unknown person.

Nothing was said. The silence was clear. A new commission, new follow-up, new records taken. And all because of the goats! Who could understand these people? Or these cursed Balkans? My father was powerful in his silence; he had learned this while reading, and he had read books enough for a few lifetimes.

"Good morning, good people," my mother began.

"God grant you well, Mother!" answered the leader.

My father looked at the man in surprise. He was an atheist. Why was he talking like this? Did he have some reason, or was it just a habit when he was talking to older people? Perhaps he felt more at liberty when there was no party member present.

My mother, with no reaction like Father's, responded, "May God help you!"

"God helps those who help themselves."

My father sensed the direction of the leader's thoughts, and he was right.

"If I am not mistaken, you had three goats," continued the leader. "Where are they?"

"We gave them away!" my mother responded, accustomed to being the first to answer when foreign soldiers burst into the house during Father's absence.

"Where did you give away the goats?" continued the leader, while those accompanying him were already looking around the courtyard and the house.

"There, we gave them away over there!" said my mother, pointing in the direction of the park.

"Where is 'there'? And, more important, to whom did you give them?"

My mother looked at my father in confusion. There was no time to gauge his reaction.

"Did you give them to Changa?"

"Yes, to Changa . . ."

"To Changa, to Changa . . . everyone gave their goats to the damned buck Changa," the leader said nervously through clenched teeth.

"And where is that blasted Changa now?" he continued.

"Changa is in the park!" we children all shouted at once.

"We're not heading down that primrose path! He's not there. He's escaped!"

126

"The goats aren't there either?" I cried out tearfully.

"No, there are no goats . . . no goats . . . none of the goats . . ."

"Who could run away with so many goats?" my brother the party member had the courage to ask.

"We are asking ourselves the same thing. And we are asking you. Where are the goats?"

"You can find out more easily than we can!" cried out my mother.

"Don't worry. We will find out everything. The city is surrounded on all sides. Not even a little chick could be saved, let alone goats . . . They can save themselves only if they can fly through the air . . . Even if they can't, they'll end up in heaven. There is no way out."

My mother, despite everything, was prepared to bring mulberry preserves and serve coffee, but the leader cut her off: "We're leaving. If you find out anything about Changa and the goats, contact the nearest police station immediately."

Somewhat heartened, we went out of the house.

Military and police patrols were moving along the streets. Everyone was looking for Changa. And the goats.

We children were first to go out, then the adults, then the entire city. Everyone was looking for Changa and the goats. But there was not a trace of them, not a sound. The commissions worked quickly. They could not find so much as a single kid. According to the commission's findings, all of them had been taken away, killed during the earlier attacks and raids; the rest had been folded into Changa's herd. This had been quickly ascertained by the police and the party. There was a new plan for the search. They now had broader objectives for searching for Changa. The major ideologues of the party and those responsible for the construction of our Socialist society, those who had instigated this goat tragedy, were looking for him. Following the phase of forced collectivization and nationalization, they had to prove that Socialism would succeed.

The critical development of the working class out of millions of goatherds, their goats now slaughtered, must succeed. Changa, with his mad parade, could change the course of history. Therefore, he must be liquidated or, even better, captured by any means.

Everyone was looking for Changa to bring back the time of the goats. The young pregnant women with weak unborn lives still in their wombs were looking for him; mothers whose milk was drying up were looking for him. Everyone was looking for Changa, but he was inside them all. He had not raised his own family; he had remained with his goats, and, through them, he connected with every family. The mothers whose children had been saved by the goats had in their houses an icon, a picture of Changa with the goats that a newspaper had once published.

Everyone quickly realized that Changa had outsmarted the republic and federal strategists who were preparing the court case of the decade in our southern republic. They hoped to realize one of their most significant plans—their plan of plans. They must demonstrate the strategic planning power of this new government. A dead Changa would not serve their purpose. Even alive, Changa already had one foot in the circle of saints and martyrs; if he were killed, Changa would definitely become a martyr. They had to be careful, very careful. The great goatherd must be captured alive. Those were the last instructions received from the republic and federal powers. Other ideas were floated—if Changa could not be captured alive, they would mount a court case against him—with a double! They would pass the blame onto him for everything they wanted and, if necessary, would even force him to testify against his goats. But that idea sank quickly. There was not a single person who did not know Changa. He had a sharp and unpredictable mind; he could not easily be outsmarted. People would see through the authorities' ruse quickly and easily, and then Changa's glory would increase, while Socialism and the party would suffer tremendous damage.

At some point, a suggestion was repeated that Changa should be judged in absentia for treason against the state. This plan was considered for a long time, every angle studied. All levels of government in the city and the republic were ready to adopt this idea, but it did not withstand the criticism at the party summit meeting and from federal authorities. There was a shrewd person there who opposed it, saying that it would unnecessarily increase Changa's reputation. Although everything up to that point regarding the city's goats had had the blessing of the federation, these higher-ups, it turned out, regularly fought among themselves. Still, the idea of trying him in absentia received the most support and was about to be adopted, so they decided to seek opinion from the other republics and districts, and even, if necessary, consult the Leader, in order to put an end to the Changa problem in the southern republic once and for all.

Responses soon arrived. The analyses were especially exhaustive from the republics with ethnically and religiously mixed populations. According to those analyses, it would not be wise to judge Changa in any fashion, either in his presence or in his absence, dead or alive, because this was guaranteed to elevate Changa. He would be the saint of the goats; he would surpass even the glory of the war heroes, surpass even the current leaders. It would not be good to charge Changa, or kill him, because no one in the whole country before Changa had gathered together, won over, loved, and united so many people of different faiths and nationalities, and in those decisive moments he had become their god.

The revolutionary strategists were afraid of the unpredictable anger of those with whom they had been victorious in the war, had carried out the Revolution, had united the people and ruled the country. Federation authorities also feared that by judging Changa they would "internationalize" the problem of the goats in the southern republic.

Reactions to the Stalin trials in several countries of the Eastern Bloc were still fresh. The world had entered the era of the Cold War. Tito was finally freed from Stalin. Yet the people would need a long time to uproot the powerful Soviet leader from their souls. They had removed Stalin's pictures from their homes, but they were frightened, and some kept the pictures hidden away, having experienced the fickleness of Balkan history.

The break with Stalin had certainly moderated our strategists' approach to the goat question and to Socialism. They would have considered themselves fortunate if both Changa and the goats had simply disappeared and no longer kicked up dust in the southern republic. But who could change the mind of the leaders of the republics?

How lucky we were that the break with Stalin had occurred and Stalinism had not developed fully in our country as it had in the neighboring Stalinist countries. We were fortunate, for example, that we broke with Stalin before the idea for the creation of museums of atheism had been realized. What if museums of atheism had been adopted here, those true concentration camps of the soul? With such museums, they planned—those cursed plans again—how to kill God in man forever, to destroy our distinctiveness and our faith.

Federation authorities were tallying various balance sheets; they pointed to other matters and other misfortunes from which we had freed ourselves through our break with Stalin. There were strong opinions not to make too big a deal of the goat question because it, too, might have been one of Stalin's ideas! But for those in favor of a radical solution to the goat question, for the destruction of all goats, no concession was possible. Furthermore, in the southern republic, inertia was stronger than it was elsewhere. If not for the thundering voices of the federation and the Leader, Stalinism would surely have continued here. Once again, they needlessly entangled the whole country in that cursed goat question.

In the federation, there were real concerns, more than ever before. The republic representatives kept silent at meetings, always waiting for some solution. It had been made explicit to them that the southern republic would in no way be included in their great plans because it was too quick or too slow in responding to basic strategic decisions.

The federal powers had believed that in the southern republic there would be the fewest problems concerning the goat question. They considered its leaders to be submissive vassals. But somehow it had not turned out that way.

And now, when the whole country needed it least of all, now when it was freed from Stalin, the people in the southern republic had dreamed up that cursed Changa. They had him cornered alive! They had let him slip through their fingers like amateurs! You could not trust them with the care of two or three goats, let alone a whole country! Instead of simply seizing him, or liquidating him, they had waited for their D-day. Amateurs! How did they not understand that cursed D-day had nothing to do with them? D-day was intended primarily to deal with the northern republics. But, strangely enough, it was easier there. The goats had been handed over with discipline. But of course, in those northern republics there were not as many who were to become the so-called working class.

20

*F*ollowing Changa's disappearance with the goats, my father was tormented by dark thoughts. He was disturbed on both a personal and a general level. He had lost one of the best friends of his life. In this person he had discovered the importance of sincerity and how simplicity in a person could be sacred. What's more, through Changa's real-life experience, my father had tested fundamental hypotheses relating to the development and evolution of the knowledge he had drawn from his vast array of books.

He who shows restraint after victory is perhaps the true victor, thought my father, inspired by the example of Changa and the goats.

After the loss of the goats, my father was sure that once again, for the nth time—who knows how many times—the victors themselves would be defeated. In fact, he regretted that this beautifully thought-out system was destined for inevitable collapse in the near future, though he did not know when.

The showdown with Changa had merely announced its imminent collapse. My father deeply lamented that some future generation of his descendants might suffer. His commitment to natural evolution, the discovery and study of its laws, here resembled one of the countless illusions prevalent among the many self-taught intellectuals in the Balkans.

He had many books about Darwin and evolution. Through his study of natural selection he wanted to comprehend all that had been lost in the Balkans due to its accursed backwardness, far behind other European nations.

He was profoundly struck that in the Balkans, each family, each community, had to rise again, start again at the beginning, build on the ruins of the preceding generations' defeats, unable to build on a natural continuity of values. From the lessons he drew from his books about the fall of the great empires in the Balkans and the fall of the Ottoman Empire, which he himself had experienced in Constantinople, he deeply lamented that his life, and the life of his family, had been overpowered first by Fascism, now by Communism.

Father was afraid that if Stalin, Janissary that he was, should also prove himself incapable of showing restraint after victory, there would be an endless display of self-aggrandizement and a reshaping of the world. Father's study of Balkan empires had led him to conclude that whenever Janissary turned emperors reached the height of their powers, to prove the immensity of their fickle souls, they would be inclined to maintain the illusion of victory at the expense of others' defeats as well as their own. This was their Janissary paradox, which had led to the most extreme cruelty in the Balkans. A deeply rooted terror ruled their souls, and that terror was transmitted to their empires with yet greater ruthlessness.

My father would then slip into his chimerical reflections about empires. All he needed was some small pretext. But this was no small pretext. It related to Changa, who was, in Father's view, a veritable Balkan anti-emperor. My father did not think of Changa solely from the perspective of dream, illusions, and myth. All our fates were bound to Changa's fate. He was our destiny. Both old and young—everyone, really—was truly alarmed about the fate of the goats. But Father's thoughts of Changa were more profound, based on what he himself had endured.

After Changa's disappearance, Father abandoned himself to his books with greater intensity. Deep, deep in the night, when sleep had sheltered all of us in its embrace and our goats tripped along in our dreams, he remained in the circle of light above his open book.

My mother seemed to follow the shadow of my father's dream. Just before she, too, fell asleep, she would come in and turn out the light; she would lay his book aside, marking the last page he had read, and would cover him lightly so as not to wake him. Sometimes, he would be half awake following the movement of her shadow along his books. After Mother had circled the room, Father was sure to fall asleep.

But now, these last few days, ever since Changa had disappeared with the goats, my father did not lift his head from his books. My mother could barely tell when he was awake and when asleep, but most of the time he did not sleep, and she did not enter the room.

Sometimes, very rarely, my father, after serious thought, would cry aloud. This happened most often in that moment between night and day, just at dawn, when he awoke abruptly. It was as if the silence within him, suspended between the poles of being and nothingness, rose from the depths of his soul, taking form in a sharp, clear voice, a cry that pierced the surrounding quiet. It seemed an outburst of all humanity, a great silent explosion of the turmoil, the blind alleys Father had encountered at the very core of his inner life. Father was a polyglot; he knew many languages, some fluently, others passively; in his life he had had many battles with words. With difficulty he had tamed even the most inaccessible in his meditations on infinity, his ideas on life's totality. Father seemed to possess his own inner language, a language of silence, in which, rather than in any spoken language, he entrusted those thoughts most difficult to express. Sometimes, though rarely, an un-expected cry, a thought still forming, would burst forth. But when Father's true cry rang out, it was surely to celebrate a victory, a triumph over words.

My mother, poor thing, would awaken in the early morning hours, anticipating Father's cries. The first time it happened, it alarmed her; she was frightened that his opened books had pushed him around some bend. She recalled how in her youth, in the town by the lake, one of her country's poets would walk along the lakeshore, talking to himself. My father had all of this poet's books in his library. So when my mother first heard my father shouting out loud, she thought that what had happened to the poet was happening to my father. Was this his last cry? God forbid! But she quickly regained her calm. My father had sensed her steps on the stairs. He stood to greet her. That had settled her. Several months later, when she heard Father's cry again, she was calm, even though, as before, she could not understand his thoughts.

This time, however, was different. My father repeated his cry, a single phrase: the Kale! My mother immediately understood that this cry was not like the earlier ones. Now he repeated the words sharply, strongly several times. She entered his study. Even though the sun's rays moved along Father's books, the lamp had not been turned off. He has not closed his eyes all night, she thought. My father greeted her with his gentle, open expression; he seemed rested, fresh. He generally never discussed with her the contents of the books he had read.

Mother took care of his books as if it were a sacred mission, but she never wanted to enter their worlds. The life of the family was her single great open book, and the days comprised the pages of the family, of her children. For the first time, Father spoke to her about his reading.

"It is as clear as day. Changa is hiding in the Kale with the goats! The only place he can be is in the fortress, nowhere else!"

21

*I*t was not difficult to discover how Father had reached the conclusion that Changa was in the fortress with the goats. After all, the most significant answers to his life's key ideas and questions were discovered in his books. After the night during which he stayed awake anxiously searching through his books, something Changa had said during their last conversation amid those books came to mind, and now he was fully convinced that he knew where Changa was.

"When animals are about to die," Changa had asked, "Why do they look for darkness?"

"I don't know," my father recalled answering, "but human beings approaching death seek light, even a ray of light, to bring lightness into the darkness of death!"

"Why is that?" Changa had persisted.

My father had then continued thoughtfully: "Contemplating death, a person expresses his powerlessness. Had he grown more accustomed to the thought of death during the course of his life, he would be less likely to seek light at the end. As death approaches, a person senses how the circle of light—his family, his people, his fatherland, the world—diminishes."

"Animals don't have a fatherland, so they don't have any light to defend!" Changa stated simply.

Evidently, neither Father nor Changa had a definitive answer, but it had been etched in the goatherd's mind: animals die in darkness.

To my father, this was a clear indication that Changa had chosen the large shelter in the fortress as a grave for himself and all the goats in the city, wishing in the end, even in death, to be worthy of their great love. My father then recalled all the books that Changa had sought in connection with the history of the fortress. Yes, Changa had clearly been fascinated by the almost mystical history of the fortress. More than once when he went with his goats along the hill up to the fortress, the goats had quickly climbed along the shaded rocky precipices where no human foot could tread, as if they had awakened some instinct passed down from their distant wild ancestors, those formidable lords of the steep Balkan peaks.

From his books, father sensed that history was one long, cloudy, uncertain dream that did not repeat nor was linked to any that had come before. There was always a new dream to dream, different from the last.

My father felt in his marrow how tragic history was when life was marked by resettlements, wars, and separations. When fate had led him here beneath the fortress, Father's dream returned, to bring to life the chronicle of the fall of the Balkan empires. This fortress was just such a monument to fallen empires.

My father had rapidly doubled, tripled the number of books he owned about the fortress. He learned that the Kale had been settled in prehistoric times, during the Neolithic and early Bronze Age, four thousand years before the Common Era; the remains of dugouts, huts, and palisades were proof of those settlements.

The Kale had remained a battleground for the changing empires; it stood like a beacon in the ocean of time. Generations of occupiers, celebrated or nameless, would fortify it, as if for the ages; they rebuilt these cyclopean stone walls that had been assembled by previous occupiers. They would establish their own order; they would haul new stone blocks or excavate them.

How could one discern the truth about the people in this time frozen in stone, or about the ephemeral nature of things, beside the eternal river flowing into the near Mediterranean Sea? First one empire was established, then a second, followed by a third. Each, in turn, would demonstrate its power through these stone formations—then disappear. And so revolved the eternal circle of life. When military commanders arrived, new occupiers of the city, the fortress always became captive to their hopes that they would rule here forever. In its shadows, imperial strategists, chroniclers, and poets stayed for days on end, lost in thought. Each laid out his vision before the exalted emperor. Their message was clear: he who rules the fortress rules the soul of the city and has an open path toward the valleys to the north and the south, on toward the sea.

Yes, consciously or not, Changa would often direct his path toward the fortress. While the goats peacefully grazed and played about the hillside, Changa walked around the fortress. He looked at its large paving stones and enormous stone blocks and thought in amazement how they had ended on this citadel, hauled from different regions.

After one such walk about the fortress, Changa asked whether my father had any books that discussed the citadel's past. Changa then discovered that the Kale, its history, and its many secrets, held great interest for my father, too; of course, my father's interest in the citadel above the city was different from Changa's. Father showed the goatherd books, old and new, about the fortress. Changa could believe almost everything in the books, but he had a hard time believing the claim that, judging by the remains of dugouts and huts, the fortress could be four thousand years old. When my father read to him what archaeologists had discovered about the age of the fortress, Changa smiled in disbelief. He had, in fact, found various artifacts while his goats grazed, but who could imagine, who could believe they were among the oldest?

Among my father's books about the fortress, Changa was most enthralled by the travel notes of Evliya Çelebi written during the Ottoman era. He was also interested in the testimonies found in Father's books by Marcellinus and Procopius, who wrote that the long rampart of the fortress with its cyclopean masonry was similar to ancient walls and dated back to the time of the Byzantine emperor Justinian I. Some of the fortress's stone blocks had been hauled from the ruins of the nearby antique city of Skupi, which had been hit by the great Balkan earthquake of 518. Then Changa saw these stone blocks with his own eyes and was convinced of the historical truth about the fortress.

My father read to Changa other books about the fortress, but he quickly lost interest in them. But when Father read him Evliya Çelebi's notes, Changa paid special heed. The description Father read seemed to him close, visible, believable. He was particularly interested in Çelebi's description of the fortress:

> From the west side flows the river Vardar. But it has a path that leads through the caves toward the water tower located on the shore of the river. On that side of the city there is a chasm, terrible as the depths of hell. There is no exit here, nor could there be. On the eastern, southern, and northern sides of the city there are deep ravines. There is a wooden bridge across the ravine on the side facing the gates. The guards sometimes raise the bridge with a winch, thereby creating a defense in front of the gates.

My father continued reading, but Changa excitedly sifted through his memories of earlier walks about the fortress either with the goats or alone. While Father read aloud, Changa would mutter words to himself, as if to verify something. My father would stop reading and remove his glasses, but Changa would beg him to continue. As Father read, Changa wanted to add what he himself knew about the history of the Kale, and in his memory, he searched most for "the path that leads through the caves toward the water tower."

Changa suspected that during its perennial and boundless floods, the river deepened the numerous caves in the bowels of the fortress. After the spring or fall floods, when the river rose, the caves were eroded further; some even merged. Throughout history, virtually every empire had wanted to settle the restless course of the great river. For a long time, their plans had not succeeded. Then, during the last century of the Ottoman Empire, with the construction of high stone levees, the river was tamed. Still, Changa was certain that the water had at one time reached the caves. He knew that some of the fortress caves had more recently been connected, paved over, and set in some order. During the Second World War, shelters had been built there, which later served other purposes. As to what other purposes—my father and Changa were not much interested. The shelters were under military and police control.

My father did not need to dig deeper in his memory for further evidence that one of the caves in the bowels of the fortress would become a grave for Changa and the goats. Once it was clear that the goats had to die, Changa wanted at least to choose for them a worthy death, in darkness, following their instinct. And Changa could do everything— both before his death and beyond.

That is what my father was thinking.

22

*T*hree days had passed since Changa's disappearance.

My father imagined that Changa was with the goats in the bowels of the Kale and that both he and the goats were now at the border of life and death.

My mother had never seen Father pace so quickly from one end of the room to the other, from the balcony to the courtyard. He could not calm down for hours on end. An idea was percolating in his mind.

My mother had never been so worried. As for us children, without our goats, with no thought of playing games, we helplessly followed Father's footsteps going past us. It seemed as though he did not even see us. He was the most worried because he carried the most responsibility. How could he not help his true friend at the moment of his greatest travail? Our family had lost the source of its tranquility: Father's confidence.

Not even during the bombardments of the city by the lake, when my father had been forced to take one of his secret trips, returning only when one occupying force or another had fortified its position, had my mother and my older brothers seen him more concerned, more worried.

When there was nowhere left for him to pace in the house, when he was fully convinced that Changa was hiding with the goats in the fortress, Father gathered his sons together to confide his big secret.

We were protected in our parents' shadow. Our family had been nearly worn out from its unpredictable migrations; we were fated always to have to accustom ourselves to new people and new customs, leaving behind our close kin, our homes, and our fields.

My father was deep in thought, as if recalling those returns from his long travels through the Balkans, undertaken to bring hope of a better life. At that time, he would end his lonely and pensive walks along the shores of the lake, where he watched the play of waves, and compare his life to the fate of those very waves, which must always begin anew their journey toward the shore.

Now he found himself by a river with no waves but a current flowing in one direction toward one end. This had led to thoughts of life's end, yet the towering fortress reminded him that hope exists. My father crossed his hands, as he did whenever he had something significant to tell us, and quietly began: "My children, three days have gone by without Changa and the goats. He is likely hiding deep inside the fortress hillside."

"With the goats?" we interrupted him in chorus.

"With the goats."

We were trembling. Our bodies were coming back to life. Life once again coursed through our veins.

Changa is alive! The goats are alive! How could there be any greater joy on this day?

Our joy came to a halt when my father quietly said, "Changa has surely chosen his death, or at least the path that leads toward death, with little hope for rescue or escape from the fortress. I have been thinking, dear children. I have thought long and hard. I have looked through my books and searched my memories for conversations with Changa. For days, we spoke at length about the fortress; I read to him from my books, and he followed the history of the fortress along each pathway, each stone.

"On the fortress, right near the top, before the military barracks, there is a deep well that leads down to the shelters. Through the well, air flows down to the shelters. The belly of the fortress hillside breathes with this air. That's how it is described in many writings about the fortress. But today, the well is nearly buried. If it is still connected with the shelters, if it is not completely blocked up, then Changa and the goats could well be alive . . ."

"That means there is hope . . ." my oldest brother said, interrupting my father.

"There is hope as long as there is life," my father continued. "Children, I have considered a possible scheme to rescue Changa and the goats, if the possibility of rescue still exists. We should try throwing food for the goats and Changa down the well."

It was clear what my father was aiming at. He was prepared to sacrifice himself, and for us to sacrifice ourselves, to save Changa and the goats.

My mother followed the conversation with alarm. She understood the magnitude of Father's sacrifice. But how could her children, with whom she had weathered so many storms and wars, her children, whom the soldiers had not taken from her, now be thrown into the mouth of the wolf, into that cursed fortress, which would devour the goats, just like Mr. Seguin's goat? That little goat, poor thing, had chosen the mountain and freedom; she had fought bravely with the wolf, but death had nabbed her nonetheless. Changa had made a similar choice with the goats. Anyone who dared to grab them from death would himself be condemned. My mother quietly begged my father to stop; there was no point in banging one's head against a wall. But the decision had ripened; it was ready to be put into effect.

That evening, my father went with my two oldest brothers to the families nearest us, and his news and plan for action spread quickly through the Goatherd Quarter, which was fully prepared to sacrifice itself for Changa and the goats.

The military and police patrols were there, but their lines had thinned; they were not everywhere, as on that first day. The authorities had increasingly accepted the fact that Changa had simply vanished. Furthermore, directives coming from the federation demanded that they were to calm the situation, not incite the masses. The army had withdrawn to its barracks, most of which were located around the fortress. That very evening, we secretly stole to the fortress in groups, unseen by the patrols.

My father carried a flashlight to illuminate the map he carried. We reached the well. It was covered with four wide boards and camouflaged with greenery. We removed them easily. Here before our eyes was the well that extended down to the shelters.

My father was pleased that the well had not been blocked up. It meant that air was likely circulating in the shelter, which meant that there was no danger that Changa and the goats had suffocated. My father flashed the light deep into the well. The ray of light did not extend far, and the well seemed bottomless. The light flashed on the stone walls, lined with spiderwebs. Through the night, together with other well-organized groups, we tossed down leafy branches for the goats and food for Changa. While the city slept soundly, groups took turns bringing leaves from all directions.

There was no reply, but we did not expect one so quickly.

At dawn the second day, a young goatherd was coming down from the fortress along one of the more remote footpaths and noticed a white liquid flowing in one of the dried streambeds. He confirmed that it was milk and called to the other goatherds: "Goat milk is flowing from the hillside! Milk from our goats!"

The news quickly spread through the Goatherd Quarter.

"Changa is alive!" "The goats are alive!"

Not even three days had passed, but the lack of goat milk was evident: the children's cheeks were already growing pale because goat milk had been the main, if not the only, source of food for many families in the Goatherd Quarter, in the city, and all across that submissive and impoverished southern republic, which was, on command, supposed to undergo immediate rapid industrial development. Why had those damned goatherds not understood this? Now it seemed that the directives themselves had been worn out. The radio had ceased broadcasting speeches against the goats with an accompaniment of revolutionary songs.

The city without Changa was a different city.

And now, all of sudden, there was milk! Milk for the children of the Goatherd Quarter!

Changa, the great Changa, even in death's embrace, was thinking of us, his people in the Goatherd Quarter, the children, the mothers, the old folk! People quickly organized to collect the milk that sprang forth from the ground. At night, some people brought food; at dawn, others collected the milk.

The people asked one another: How could milk be flowing from the fortress? Could Changa be milking hundreds of goats by himself? Or were the goats pouring the milk into the streams themselves? How many secrets were held in the belly of the fortress!

In the city, people believed that this miracle could bring other miracles as well. Hope returned. Changa had to triumph. Another day, two, three . . . perhaps an order would arrive from the Federation. Surely, the Federal government members would take pity on us, now that God himself had taken pity on the poor folk of the Goatherd Quarter. Stalin was gone. Without him, we were now our own people, right? They could make a small decision or two on their own. If the members of the Federation had been aware, if after all the prayers invoked by the mothers in private and in public, the truth about the goats had reached the Supreme Leader, surely they would have yielded. It was clear: hope was returning to the Goatherd Quarter.

My father was too well acquainted with the nature of Stalinism to allow himself to be optimistic about the fate of Changa and the goats.

Even after the Stalinist era, it was difficult to change things, despite the constant pronouncements that everything was being carried out in the name of progress, change, and the people's happiness.

This would later lead to the birth of the omnipresent slogan: "Man is the greatest wealth of Socialism." No, there could be no turning back! And when errors were made, especially in the countries of the Eastern Bloc, there was no correction, no looking back, no regression. Mistakes were never acknowledged. And in those other Socialist countries where Stalinism remained even after the disappearance of Stalin, his legacy bore fruit, fertilized by local fantasies. They erected walls at their borders for no purpose, and the highest were in the Balkans; they built new concrete bunkers; they destroyed the old temples of worship—all in the name of man's happiness! As if there could be a center charged with planning the happiness of each and every person. And that center never made a mistake!

My father knew quite well that there was no "reverse" in Socialism! And that thought frightened him most of all as he regarded the fate of Changa and the goats. They were to be sacrificed. There was to be a sacrifice of nannies and billies, a sacrifice of childhoods, and a sacrifice of Changa. Even now, when it was certain that Changa and the goats were still alive, when a bridge had been built between the death Changa had chosen and possible life, when hope had returned once again to these poor suffering people, my father became more downhearted, broken, because he could not accomplish the decisive step. No such step was possible. No matter where he went, no matter whom in the government he would try to convince—and he had no access to the party—he would quickly come under suspicion; they would question him, open new wounds in those still raw from the recent past. Who was he, after all? A newcomer from a foreign country, a hostile one at that. And was he, an immigrant, to tell them what to do?

My mother tried in vain to convince him to forget the goats and Changa before he dragged everyone into the abyss. Let those who were to be sacrificed, be sacrificed. What could we do? My father remained withdrawn in the fortress of his thoughts beside his silent books; now even they held no answers and had been drained of meaning. Earlier, when life had been difficult for him, these books seemed to turn the pages themselves, but then there had been a way out, a new page to turn. But now . . . ?

Not even a half hour had passed since my father had sent my two older brothers to the fortress for their turn to bring food when the metal handle knocked three times against the metal ball on the courtyard gate. Who could that be? My brothers had just gone and were to return in exactly three hours. But those three knocks were unambiguous; that was clearly my brothers' signal. We all leaped from our places. My mother got to the door first. She was relieved when she saw her two sons; for her, what they would say was not the most important thing. My father quickly, nervously, waited to hear their explanation.

"The fortress is surrounded on all sides by the army and police. There is even a guard at the head of the Wooden Bridge. No one can get near the fortress from any side!" my oldest brother said quickly.

My father was drenched in sweat. My mother was the most calm. We were there together, but everything else . . .

Fear, which we thought had departed after that small ray of hope, entered our house and the Goatherd Quarter once again. If someone had denounced Changa, it would not be long before they knocked on our door, too, on the doors of all the houses in the quarter. Now each house, like the Kale, had become a fortress of fear. New waves of concern played unwittingly across the creases of Mother's forehead. Once fear had entered the house, it would come and go across her face. We did not close our eyes all night. We waited for my father and my older brothers to be taken away. But no one came.

In the morning, my mother, as usual, was first to open the courtyard gate. The sun crossed the threshold. The street was peaceful, empty. She stepped out and soon found herself on the quay, facing the river embankment, under the shadow of the tall poplars. On the opposite shore of the river, on the slopes of the hill on which the Kale rose, stood scattered rows of armed soldiers. The fortress was surrounded, but there was no movement of the military units.

From the first goatherds she met, Mother learned that not a single goatherd had been apprehended and no home invaded. But during the night, wondrous things had occurred on the Kale. No one could figure it all out, but by noon my father was able to piece together a complete mosaic of the nighttime events.

The possibility that someone had informed on Changa was dismissed immediately. There was a holy brotherhood among the goatherds. Never in such a short time had such great differences between these people been brushed aside so quickly and turned into a shared belief. There could be no informers among the goatherds.

My father had imagined before, but now had concrete proof, that the central figures in the city's war against the goats had considered the possibility that Changa might hide himself in the fortress. That theory had not been fully developed, however, because other theories had been more persuasive. Still, more as a routine matter, they decided to check the shelters below the fortress. And what should they see? All the entrances to the shelters had been walled up! And before each door, mounds of goat dung. An overpowering stench was spreading. Real alarm rose among the central authorities.

During the night, the question burned; the goat question had been rekindled. Telephone calls were made, telegrams sent in every direction, the leaders awakened. They did not want to disturb the federal leaders. There, key people had wanted to calm the situation, but who could calm the republic leaders now, especially those avowed enemies of the goats? They organized quickly; they sought permission to put a plan in place, to complete the job: *Operation Kale*. But who could have imagined that Changa would wall up the doors to the shelters, shutting off all approaches to the heart of the fortress? They used explosives. They opened one wall, but there was another behind it. More explosions. A third wall, and between the walls: huge piles of goat excrement. That's the greeting Changa had arranged for his pursuers.

They blasted through all the walls and found themselves in a labyrinth of goat dung. They could not make sense of what they saw: closed, walled-up doors and fresh branches! Not a single one of them had thought of the well at the top of the fortress. Torches were burning, kept alive by the draft blowing between the opened doors and the well. They were looking for Changa and the goats. There were shouts to surrender, but of Changa and the goats there was no trace, no sound.

The pursuers soon found themselves in front of a huge cauldron connected by pipes to passageways out from the mountain. The milky streams were now dried up. The soldiers and the police, together with representatives of the government and the party, especially those responsible for the goat question, searched in vain through the night for the goats and for Changa. They were in radio communication with the republic leadership located on the slopes of the other, larger hill. At dawn, the command was given to halt the search through the underground shelters.

Even those on duty at the federal level were informed. The authorities there did not react; they did not want to wake the Leader to inform him about this regional chaos. After all, he had not been involved with the goat problem; that had fallen to the main ideologue of the party and principal strategist of the regime. Besides, he was not there; he was back in his northern Yugoslav republic. To contact him at this time was unthinkable.

So the night hunt for Changa and the goats continued in the bowels of the fortress. They decided to ignite the branches, the leaves, and the goat dung to achieve their ultimate goal by suffocating Changa and the goats if they were alive. No sooner said than done. But then someone noticed smoke pouring out of the well, and they realized that the well-organized goatherds must have been sending down food to Changa and the goats. Who could bring an end to this united tribe of goatherds? Every inch of the shelters was searched. Changa was not there. Evidently, he had simply vanished with the goats. He had either fallen through the earth or performed some new trick.

In the morning, the republic leadership sent a final dispatch to the federation: "Changa has been liquidated together with all the goats! There is no longer a goat problem in the southern republic. That is certain. Now, after successful collectivization, it will be possible to move with rapid steps toward industrialization. It will be difficult to educate these goatherds overnight; the goats are never going to disappear from their memory, but in the end, they will surely understand the truth about Communism. They have no choice; they have no other future."

Federation authorities could breathe easily at last.

The most significant strategic question concerning the development of the southern republic had been decided. There remained the literacy campaign, but according to projections, that should not pose a problem as great as, for example, electrification. But the goats—the goats had been a huge obstacle on the road toward Communism.

Now all roads were open. However, the goat question was to disturb souls in the republics and the federation once more. Although the devil, that goat-devil, may not dig or plow, he was here. After the opening of the country and the end of Stalinism, no matter how much they wanted to push the goat question, and the unfinished and unsuccessful collectivization, into the background, especially after the split between Tito and Stalin and the exclusion of Yugoslavia from the Eastern Bloc and its subsequent turn toward the West, journalists began to arrive more frequently to see what was happening behind the Iron Curtain. Now that "the goat question had been laid to rest, these cursed Western journalist busybodies wanted to revive it." The federation was at first reserved toward these foreign journalists, but in the end, it had to make concessions. The journalists were most interested in visiting the southern republic. For the first time since the war, there were journalists from international news agencies whose names we had heard constantly on our radio stations. After the war, there were also consulates in the city, which, through their channels, spread the truth about the time of the goats. Changa was a true hero in these bulletins. The foreign journalists had all the information they needed about him and the goats, but now, according to the authorities, they were poking their noses where they did not belong. Some of the journalists even found their way to my father. But my mother was frightened when she saw them with their beards and cameras, and she did not let them into the house, telling them that she was home alone. She told them to come back later, but they had already spoken with some of the other goatherds and did not return. My father, when he learned what my mother had done, looked at her in surprise but told her that she had done the right thing. He did not want too much to be known about him. Others could give statements more freely.

A friend who prepared state bulletins summarizing what the foreign press was writing about the country hired my father to translate, or at least help translate, articles from the foreign press. While also digging deeper into the mists of his conscience, Father was quickly able to learn more of the truth about the end of Changa and the goats. He eagerly read the headlines of articles published in the widely circulated Western papers and noted their contents. He read headlines such as "The Pharaoh Changa Died in His Pyramid with the Goats," "Changa Suffocated in Military Shelters with His Faithful Goats," "Changa Discovered Unknown Exits from the Fortress," "In the Balkans, Following the Killings in the War, the Killings and Trials against the Goats Continue," "There Is No Peace in the Balkans."

Epilogue

$\mathcal{M}$y father had difficulty making peace with his loss.

We children and Mother were equally worried by the loss of Father's tranquility. Of course, we never got over the loss of our goats. In our childhood, our souls carried a raw wound that never fully healed.

When my father turned once again to his books, Mother could finally relax. She believed that the family would now live as it had in the days of its former tranquility. My father continued to study his books and documents to complete his *History of the Empires of the Balkans through the History of Their Collapse.* He kept changing the working title of the book. He knew that he would never complete it, but this is how he preserved the endless flow of his Balkan illusions. Now he appeared to set aside his most important books in order to write down living testimony demonstrating the inevitable fall of Stalin's empire. After the harsh settling of accounts with the goats and the goatherds (not destined to become the working class), after collectivization and its tragic consequences, after the reckoning with religions and the construction of museums dedicated to atheism throughout the whole empire, my father was convinced of the imminent collapse of Stalinism.

The city regained its calm after the stormy time of the goats. Nobody dared to mention goats, let alone keep them. The laws that were introduced were harsh, and they accomplished what they were intended to accomplish.

When Father set aside his books, he would go out for his customary stroll. He would head toward the quay and then down to the river. He would cross the Wooden Bridge, glancing to the right at the neoclassical building of the theater with its caryatids protecting one another and a past regime. Then he would walk through the Jewish Quarter and take the path toward the western foothills of the Kale. He would stop in front of the entrance to the shelters. Through the open vents in the metal doors he peered into the eyes of the darkness, into the eyes of thousands of goats. Then his path led him to the water tower by the river. Here, he had discovered an abandoned cistern—deep, dark, impenetrable. He would draw near it. Sometimes, when he was exhausted from a night of reading, he could hear a gurgling sound bubbling up from the depths of the cistern.

My father could never quite determine whether Changa emitted this grotesque laughter to mock his pursuers and the entire Stalinist era or to send a greeting to him alone, his friend.

In his daydreams, my father imagined that the gurgling in the cistern marked the course of water flowing toward the underground shelters in the caves. That was nearly impossible, worthy of science fiction. But after the disappearance of Changa and the goats in the bowels of the fortress, Father needed a haven for his restless thoughts. After listening a long while to the gurgling of the cistern, that indecipherable language from the innermost core of the mountain, my father quickly returned along his same route. He went directly to his books and continued to turn the pages, to study, to search through his books and his memory.

His thoughts made their way to the large lake on whose shores he had spent his early childhood and youth; he held on to the hope that he would return there in his old age. Futile Balkan hopes! When he was young, he had been tormented by the desire to know whether under that lake and the lake on the other side of the mountain the waters joined, creating numerous caves, as claimed by tradition and suggested in scientific writings. He had had no answer then beside the lake, just as he had none now beside the cistern by the river, from whose depths he could hear Changa's call and the bleating of the goats. In the course of time, he stopped going to the cistern, though Changa continued to rise and set in his memories.

From the recesses of his consciousness, Father let go of his last theory that Changa and the goats had discovered an underground exit from the fortress to this cistern. He finally stopped thinking of the cistern, that forgotten tomb of time past. For my father, this is where the riddle of Changa and his goats came to an end. For my mother, this marked Father's happy return from books into life. For us children, it marked the ending of the most beautiful time in the world, the time of the goats.